NESS

'What a very, very
LUCKY
person you are.

Spread out before you are the
FINEST and **FUNNIEST**
words from the finest and funniest writer
the past century ever knew. '

Stephen Fry

LOCH NESS

'Mr Wodehouse's
IDYLLIC WORLD CAN NEVER STALE.
He will continue to release future generations from captivity
that may be more irksome than our own. He has made a
world for us to live in and delight in'

Evelyn Waugh

'**THE ULTIMATE IN COMFORT READING**
because nothing bad ever happens in P.G. Wodehouse land. Or
even if it does, it's always sorted out by the end of the book. For as
long as I'm immersed in a P.G. Wodehouse book, it's possible to
keep the real world at bay and live in a far, far nicer, funnier
one where happy endings are the order of the day'

Marian Keyes

'You should read Wodehouse when you're well
and when you're poorly; when you're travelling,
and when you're not; when you're feeling clever, and when
you're feeling utterly dim. Wodehouse
ALWAYS LIFTS YOUR SPIRITS,
no matter how high they happen to be already'

Lynne Truss

'P.G. Wodehouse remains the greatest chronicler of
A CERTAIN KIND OF ENGLISHNESS,
that no one else has ever captured quite so sharply, or with
quite as much wit and affection'

Julian Fellowes

'Not only the funniest English novelist who
ever wrote but one of our finest stylists.
His world is **PERFECT**, his stories are
PERFECT, his writing is **PERFECT**.
What more is there to be said?'

Susan Hill

Pelham Grenville Wodehouse (always known as 'Plum') wrote about seventy novels and some three hundred short stories over 73 years. He is widely recognised as the greatest 20th-century writer of humour in the English language.

Wodehouse mixed the high culture of his classical education with the popular slang of the suburbs in both England and America, becoming a 'cartoonist of words'. Drawing on the antics of a near-contemporary world, he placed his Drones, Earls, Ladies (including draconian aunts and eligible girls) and Valets, in a recently vanished society, whose reality is transformed by his remarkable imagination into something timeless and enduring.

Perhaps best known for the escapades of Bertie Wooster and Jeeves, Wodehouse also created the world of Blandings Castle, home to Lord Emsworth and his cherished pig, the Empress of Blandings. His stories include gems concerning the irrepressible and disreputable Ukridge; Psmith, the elegant socialist; the ever-so-slightly-unscrupulous Fifth Earl of Ickenham, better known as Uncle Fred; and those related by Mr Mulliner, the charming raconteur of The Angler's Rest, and the Oldest Member at the Golf Club.

Wodehouse collaborated with a variety of partners on straight plays and worked principally alongside Guy Bolton on providing the lyrics and script for musical comedies with such composers as George Gershwin, Irving Berlin and Cole Porter. He liked to say that the royalties for 'Just My Bill', which Jerome Kern incorporated into *Showboat*, were enough to keep him in tobacco and whisky for the rest of his life.

In 1936 he was awarded the Mark Twain Prize for 'having made an outstanding and lasting contribution to the happiness of the world'. He was made a Doctor of Letters by Oxford University in 1939 and in 1975, aged 93, he was knighted by Queen Elizabeth II. He died shortly afterwards, on St Valentine's Day.

To have created so many characters that require no introduction places him in a very select group of writers, led by Shakespeare and Dickens.

18/06/2023

P. G. WODEHOUSE

Aunts Aren't Gentlemen

3 800

arrow books

17 19 20 18 16

Arrow Books
20 Vauxhall Bridge Road
London SW1V 2SA

Arrow Books is part of the Penguin Random House group of companies
whose addresses can be found at global.penguinrandomhouse.com

Penguin
Random House
UK

Copyright © The Trustees of the Wodehouse Estate

First published in Great Britain by Barrie & Jenkins Ltd in 1974
First published by Arrow Books in 2008

www.penguin.co.uk
www.wodehouse.co.uk

A CIP catalogue record for this book is available from the British Library.

ISBN 9780099513971

Typeset by SX Composing DTP, Rayleigh, Essex
Printed and bound in Great Britain by Clays Ltd, Elcograf S.p.A.

Penguin Random House is committed to a sustainable future
for our business, our readers and our planet. This book is made
from Forest Stewardship Council® certified paper.

MIX
Paper from
responsible sources
FSC® C018179

Aunts Aren't
Gentlemen

CHAPTER ONE

My attention was drawn to the spots on my chest when I was in my bath, singing, if I remember rightly, the Toreador song from the opera *Carmen*. They were pink in colour, rather like the first faint flush of dawn, and I viewed them with concern. I am not a fussy man, but I do object to being freckled like a pard, as I once heard Jeeves describe it, a pard, I take it, being something in the order of one of those dogs beginning with d.

'Jeeves,' I said at the breakfast table, 'I've got spots on my chest.'

'Indeed, sir?'

'Pink.'

'Indeed, sir?'

'I don't like them.'

'A very understandable prejudice, sir. Might I enquire if they itch?'

'Sort of.'

'I would not advocate scratching them.'

'I disagree with you. You have to take a firm line with spots. Remember what the poet said.'

'Sir?'

'The poet Ogden Nash. The poem he wrote defending the practice of scratching. Who was Barbara Frietchie, Jeeves?'

'A lady of some prominence in the American war between the States, sir.'

'A woman of strong character? One you could rely on?'

'So I have always understood, sir.'

'Well, here's what the poet Nash wrote. "I'm greatly attached to Barbara Frietchie. I'll bet she scratched when she was itchy." But I shall not be content with scratching. I shall place myself in the hands of a competent doctor.'

'A very prudent decision, sir.'

The trouble was that, except for measles when I was just starting out, I've always been so fit that I didn't know any doctors. Then I remembered that my American pal, Tipton Plimsoll, with whom I had been dining last night to celebrate his betrothal to Veronica, only daughter of Colonel and Lady Hermione Wedge of Blandings Castle, Shropshire, had mentioned one who had once done him a bit of good. I went to the telephone to get his name and address.

Tipton did not answer my ring immediately, and when he did it was to reproach me for waking him at daybreak. But after he had got this off his chest and I had turned the conversation to mine he was most helpful. It was with the information I wanted that I returned to Jeeves.

'I've just been talking to Mr Plimsoll, Jeeves, and everything is straight now. He bids me lose no time in establishing contact with a medico of the name of E. Jimpson Murgatroyd. He says if I want a sunny practitioner who will prod me in the ribs with his stethoscope and tell me an anecdote about two Irishmen named Pat and Mike and then another about two Scotsmen named Mac and Sandy, E. Jimpson is not my man, but if what I'm after is someone to cure my spots, he unquestionably is, as he knows his spots from A to Z and has been treating them since he was so high. It seems that Tipton had the same trouble not long ago and Murgatroyd fixed him up in no time. So while I am getting out of these clothes into something more spectacular will you give him a buzz and make an appointment.'

When I had doffed the sweater and flannels in which I had breakfasted, Jeeves informed me that E. Jimpson could see me at eleven, and I thanked him and asked him to tell the garage to send the car round at ten-forty-five.

'Somewhat earlier than that, sir,' he said, 'if I might make the suggestion. The traffic. Would it not be better to take a cab?'

'No, and I'll tell you why. After I've seen the doc, I thought I might drive down to Brighton and get a spot of sea air. I don't suppose the traffic will be any worse than usual, will it?'

'I fear so, sir. A protest march is taking place this morning.'

'What, again? They seem to have them every hour on the hour these days, don't they?'

'They are certainly not infrequent, sir.'

'Any idea what they're protesting about?'

'I could not say, sir. It might be one thing or it might be another. Men are suspicious, prone to discontent. Subjects still loathe the present Government.'

'The poet Nash?'

'No, sir. The poet Herrick.'

'Pretty bitter.'

'Yes, sir.'

'I wonder what they had done to him to stir him up like that. Probably fined him five quid for failing to abate a smoky chimney.'

'As to that I have no information, sir.'

Seated in the old sports model some minutes later and driving to keep my tryst with E. Jimpson Murgatroyd, I was feeling singularly light-hearted for a man with spots on his chest. It was a beautiful morning, and it wouldn't have taken much to make me sing Tra-la as I bowled along. Then I came abaft of the protest march and found myself becalmed. I leaned back and sat observing the proceedings with a kindly eye.

CHAPTER TWO

Whatever these bimbos were protesting about, it was obviously something they were taking to heart rather. By the time I had got into their midst not a few of them had decided that animal cries were insufficient to meet the case and were saying it with bottles and brickbats, and the police who were present in considerable numbers seemed not to be liking it much. It must be rotten being a policeman on these occasions. Anyone who has got a bottle can throw it at you, but if you throw it back, the yell of police brutality goes up and there are editorials in the papers next day.

But the mildest cop can stand only so much, and it seemed to me, for I am pretty shrewd in these matters, that in about another shake of a duck's tail hell's foundations would be starting to quiver. I hoped nobody would scratch my paint.

Leading the procession, I saw with surprise, was a girl I knew. In fact, I had once asked her to marry me. Her name was Vanessa Cook, and I had met her at a cocktail party, and such was her radiant beauty that it was only a couple of minutes after I had brought her a martini and one of those little sausages on sticks that I was saying to myself, 'Bertram, this is a good thing. Push it along.' And in due season I suggested a merger. But apparently I was not the type, and no business resulted.

This naturally jarred the Wooster soul a good deal at the moment, but reviewing the dead past now I could see that my guardian angel had been on the job all right and had known what was good for me. I mean, radiant beauty is all very well, but it isn't everything. What sort of a married life would I have had with the little woman perpetually going on protest marches and expecting me to be at her side throwing bottles at the constabulary? It made me shudder to think what I might have let myself in for if I had been a shade more fascinating. Taught me a lesson, that did – viz. never to lose faith in your guardian angel, because these guardian angels are no fools.

Vanessa Cook was accompanied by a beefy bloke without a hat in whom I recognized another old acquaintance, O. J. (Orlo) Porter to wit, who had been on the same staircase with me at Oxford. Except for borrowing an occasional cup of sugar from one another and hulloing when we met on the stairs we had never been really close, he being a prominent figure at the Union, where I was told he made fiery far-to-the-left speeches, while I was more the sort that is content just to exist beautifully.

Nor did we get together in our hours of recreation, for his idea of a good time was to go off with a pair of binoculars and watch birds, a thing that has never appealed to me. I can't see any percentage in it. If I meet a bird, I wave a friendly hand at it, to let it know that I wish it well, but I don't want to crouch behind a bush observing its habits. So, as I say, Orlo Porter was in no sense a buddy of mine, but we had always got on all right and I still saw him every now and then.

Everybody at Oxford had predicted a pretty hot political

future for him, but it hadn't got started yet. He was now in the employment of the London and Home Counties Insurance Company and earned the daily b. by talking poor saps – I was one of them – into taking out policies for larger amounts than they would have preferred. Making fiery far-to-the-left speeches naturally fits a man for selling insurance, enabling him to find the *mot juste* and enlarging the vocabulary. I for one had been corn before his sickle, as the expression is.

The bottle-throwing had now reached the height of its fever and I was becoming more than ever nervous about my paint, when all of a sudden there occurred an incident which took my mind off that subject. The door of the car opened and what the papers call a well-nourished body, male, leaped in and took a seat beside me. Gave me a bit of a start, I don't mind admitting, the Woosters not being accustomed to this sort of thing so soon after breakfast. I was about to ask to what I was indebted for the honour of this visit, when I saw that what I had drawn was Orlo Porter and I divined that after the front of the procession had passed from my view he must have said or done something which London's police force could not overlook, making instant flight a must. His whole demeanour was that of the hart that pants for cooling streams when heated in the chase.

Well, you don't get cooling streams in the middle of the metropolis, but there was something I could do to give his morale a shot in the arm. I directed his attention to the Drones Club scarf lying on the seat, at the same time handing him my hat. He put them on, and the rude disguise proved effective. Various rozzers came along, but they were looking for a man without a hat and he was definitely hatted, so they passed us by. Of course, I was bareheaded, but one look at me was enough to tell them that this polished boulevardier could not possibly be the dubious character they were after. And a few minutes later the crowd had melted.

'Drive on, Wooster,' said Orlo. 'Get a move on, blast you.'

He spoke irritably, and I remembered that he had always been an irritable chap, as who would not have been, having to go through life with a name like Orlo,and peddling insurance when he had hoped to electrify the House of Commons with his molten eloquence. I took no umbrage, accordingly, if umbrage is the thing you take when people start ordering you about, making allowances for his state of mind. I drove on, and he said 'Phew' and removed a bead of persp. from the brow.

I hardly knew what to do for the best. He was still panting like a hart, and some fellows when panting like harts enjoy telling you all about it, while others prefer a tactful silence. I decided to take a chance.

'Spot of trouble?' I said.

'Yes.'

'Often the way during these protest marches. What happened?'

'I socked a cop.'

I could see why he was a bit emotional. Socking cops is a thing that should be done sparingly, if at all. I resumed the quiz.

'Any particular reason? Or did it just seem a good idea at the time?'

He gnashed a tooth or two. He was a red-headed chap, and my experience of the red-headed is that you can always expect high blood pressure from them in times of stress. The first Queen Elizabeth had red hair, and look what she did to Mary Queen of Scots.

'He was arresting the woman I love.'

I could understand how this might well have annoyed him. I have loved a fair number of women in my time, though it always seems to wear off after a while, and I should probably have drained the bitter cup a bit if I had seen any of them pinched by the police.

'What had she done?'

'She was heading the procession with me and shouting a good deal as always happens on these occasions when the emotions of a generous girl are stirred. He told her to stop shouting. She said this was a free country and she was entitled to shout as much as she pleased. He said not if she was shouting the sort of things she was shouting, and she called him a Cossack and socked him. Then he arrested her, and I socked him.'

A pang of pity for the stricken officer passed through me. Orlo, as I have said, was well nourished, and Vanessa was one of those large girls who pack a hefty punch. A cop socked by both of them would have entertained no doubt as to his having been in a fight.

But this was not what was occupying my thoughts. At the words 'she was heading the procession with me' I had started visibly. It seemed to me that, coupled with that 'woman I love' stuff, they could mean only one thing.

'Good Lord,' I said. 'Is Vanessa Cook the woman you love?'

'She is.'

'Nice girl,' I said, for there is never any harm in giving the old salve. 'And, of course, radiant-beauty-wise in the top ten.'

A moment later I was regretting that I had pitched it so strong, for the effect on Orlo was most unpleasant. His eyes bulged, at the same time flashing, as if he were on the verge of making a fiery far-to-the-left speech.

'You know her?' he said, and his voice was low and guttural, like that of a bulldog which has attempted to swallow a chump chop and only got it down half-way.

I saw that I would do well to watch my step, for it was evident that what I have heard Jeeves call the green-eyed monster that doth mock the meat it feeds on was beginning to feel the rush of life beneath its keel. You never know what may happen when the g.-e.m. takes over.

'Slightly,' I said. 'Very slightly. We just met for a moment at some cocktail party or other.'

'That was all?'

'That was all.'

'You were not – how shall I put it? – in any sense intimate?'

'No, no. Simply on Good-morning-good-morning-lovely-morning-is-it-not terms if I happened to run into her in the street.'

'Nothing more?'

'Nothing more.'

I had said the right thing. He went off the boil, and when he next spoke, it was without bulldog and chump chop effects.

'You call her a nice girl. That puts in a nutshell my own opinion of her.'

'And she, I imagine, thinks highly of you?'

'Correct.'

'You're engaged, possibly?'

'Yes.'

'Many happy returns.'

'But we can't get married because of her father.'

'He objects?'

'Strongly.'

'But surely you don't have to have Father's consent in these enlightened days?'

A look of pain came into his face and he writhed like an electric fan. It was plain that my words had touched a sore s.

'You do if he is trustee for your money and you don't make enough at your job to marry on. My Uncle Joe left me enough to get married to twenty girls. He was Vanessa's father's partner in one of those big provision businesses. But I can't touch it because he made old Cook my trustee, and Cook refuses to part.'

'Why?'

'He disapproves of my political views. He says he has no intention of encouraging any damned Communists.'

I think at this juncture I may have looked askance at him a bit. I hadn't realized that that was what he was, and it rather shocked me, because I'm not any too keen on Communists. However, he was my guest, so to speak, so I merely said that that must have been unpleasant, and he said Yes, very unpleasant, adding that only Cook's grey hairs had saved him from getting plugged in the eye, which shows that it's not such a bad thing to let your hair go grey.

'And in addition to disliking my political views he considers that I have led Vanessa astray. He has heard about her going on these protest marches, and he considers me responsible. But for me, he says, she would never have done such a thing, and that if she ever made herself conspicuous and got her name in the papers, she would come straight home and stay there. He has a big house in the country with a stable of racehorses, as he can well afford to after his years of grinding the faces of the widow and the orphan.'

I could have corrected him here, pointing out that you don't grind people's faces by selling them pressed beef and potato chips at a lower price than they would be charged elsewhere, but, as I say, he was my guest, so I refrained. I was conscious of a passing thought that Vanessa Cook would not be remaining long in London now that she had developed this habit of socking policemen, but I did not share this with Orlo Porter, not wishing to rub salt into the wound.

'But let's not talk about it any more,' he said, closing the subject with a bang. 'You can drop me anywhere round here. Thanks for the ride.'

'Don't mention it.'

'Where are you going?'

'Harley Street, to see a doctor. I've got spots on my chest.'

The effect of this disclosure was rather remarkable. A keen go-getter look came into his face, and I could see that Orlo Porter the lover had been put in storage for the time being, his place taken by Orlo Porter the zealous employee of the London and Home Counties Insurance Company.

'Spots?' he said.

'Pink,' I said.

'Pink spots,' he said. 'That's serious. You'd better take out a policy with me.'

I reminded him that I had already done so. He shook his head.

'Yes, yes, yes, but that was only for accidents. What you must have now is a life policy, and most fortunately,' he said, drawing papers from his pocket like a conjuror taking rabbits from a hat, 'I happen to have one on me. Sign here, Wooster,' he said, this time producing a fountain pen.

And such was his magnetism that I signed there. He registered approval.

'You have done the wise thing, Wooster. Whatever the doctor may tell you when you see him, however brief your span of life, it will be a comfort to you to know that your widow and the little ones are provided for. Drop me here, Wooster.'

I dropped him, and drove on to Harley Street.

CHAPTER THREE

In spite of being held up by the protest march I was a bit early for my appointment, and was informed on arrival that the medicine man was tied up for the moment with another gentleman. I took a seat and was flitting idly through the pages of an *Illustrated London News* of the previous December when the door of E. Jimpson Murgatroyd's private lair opened and there emerged an elderly character with one of those square, empire-building faces, much tanned as if he was accustomed to sitting out in the sun without his parasol. Seeing me, he drank me in for a while and then said 'Hullo', and conceive my emotion when I recognized him as Major Plank the explorer and Rugby football aficionado, whom I had last seen at his house in Gloucestershire when he was accusing me of trying to get five quid out of him under false pretences. A groundless charge, I need scarcely say, self being as pure as the driven snow, if not purer, but things had got a bit difficult and the betting was that they would become difficult now. I sat waiting for him to denounce me and was wondering what the harvest would be, when he spoke, to my astonishment, in the most bonhomous way, as if we were old buddies.

'We've met before. I never forget a face. Isn't your name Allen or Allenby or Alexander or something?'

'Wooster,' I said, relieved to the core. I had been anticipating a painful scene. He clicked his tongue. 'I could have sworn it was something beginning with Al. It's this malaria of mine. Picked it up in Equatorial Africa, and it affects my memory. So you've changed your name, have you? Secret enemies after you?'

'No, no secret enemies.'

'That's generally why one changes one's name. I had to change mine that time I shot the chief of the 'Mgombis. In self-defence, of course, but that made no difference to his widows and surviving relatives who were looking for me. If they had caught me, they would have roasted me alive over a slow fire, which is a thing one always wants to avoid. But I baffled them. Plank was the man they were trying to contact, and it never occurred to them that somebody called George Bernard Shaw could be the chap they were after. They are not very bright in those parts. Well, Wooster, how have you been since we last met? Pretty bobbish?'

'Oh, fine, thanks, except that I've got spots on my chest.'

'Spots? That's bad. How many?'

I said I had not actually taken a census, but there were quite a few, and he shook his head gravely.

'Might be bubonic plague or possibly sprue or schistosomiasis. One of my native bearers got spots on his chest, and we buried him before sundown. Had to. Delicate fellows, these native bearers, though you wouldn't think so to look at them. Catch everything that's going around – sprue, bubonic plague, schistosomiasis, jungle fever, colds in the head – the lot. Well, Wooster, it's been nice seeing you again. I would ask you to lunch, but I have a train to catch. I'm off to the country.'

He left me, as you may imagine, in something of a twitter. Bertram Wooster, as is well known, is intrepid and it takes a lot to scare the pants off him. But his talk of native bearers who had to be buried before sundown had caused me not a little anxiety. Nor did the first sight of E. Jimpson Murgatroyd do anything to put me at my ease. Tipton had warned me that he was a gloomy old buster, and a gloomy old buster was what he proved to be. He had sad, brooding eyes and long whiskers, and his resemblance to a frog which had been looking on the dark side since it was a slip of a tadpole sent my spirits right down into the basement.

However, as so often happens when you get to know a fellow better, he turned out to be not nearly as pessimistic a Gawd-help-us as he appeared to be at first sight. By the time he had weighed me and tied that rubber thing round my biceps and felt my pulse and tapped me all over like a whiskered woodpecker he had quite brightened up and words of good cheer were pouring out of him like ginger beer from a bottle.

'I don't think you have much to worry about,' he said.

'You don't?' I said, considerably bucked up. 'Then it isn't sprue or schistosomiasis?'

'Of course it is not. What gave you the idea it might be?'

'Major Plank said it might. The chap who was in here before me.'

'You shouldn't listen to people, especially Plank. We were at school together. Barmy Plank we used to call him. No, the spots are of no importance. They will disappear in a few days.'

'Well, that's a relief,' I said, and he said he was glad I was pleased.

'But,' he added.

This chipped a bit off my *joie de vivre*.

'But what?'

He was looking like a minor prophet about to rebuke the sins of the people – it was the whiskers that did it mostly, though the eyebrows helped. I forgot to mention that he had bushy eyebrows – and I could see that this was where I got the bad news.

'Mr Wooster,' he said, 'you are a typical young man about town.'

'Oh, thanks,' I responded, for it sounded like a compliment, and one always likes to say the civil thing.

'And like all young men of your type you pay no attention to your health. You drink too much.'

'Only at times of special revelry. Last night, for instance, I was helping a pal to celebrate the happy conclusion of love's young dream, and it may be that I became a mite polluted, but that rarely happens. One Martini Wooster, some people call me.'

He paid no attention to my frank manly statement, but carried on regardless.

'You smoke too much. You stay up too late at night. You don't get enough exercise. At your age you ought to be playing Rugby football for the old boys of your school.'

'I didn't go to a Rugger school.'

'Where did you go?'

'Eton.'

'Oh,' he said, and he said it as if he didn't think much of Eton. 'Well, there you are. You do all the things I have said. You abuse your health in a hundred ways. Total collapse may come at any moment.'

'At any moment?' I quavered.

'At any moment. Unless –'

'Unless?' Now, I felt, he was talking.

'Unless you give up this unwholesome London life. Go to the country. Breathe pure air. Go to bed early. And get plenty of exercise. If you do not do this, I cannot answer for the consequences.'

He had shaken me. When a doctor, even if whiskered, tells you he cannot answer for the consequences, that's strong stuff. But I was not dismayed, because I had spotted a way of following his advice without anguish. Bertram Wooster is like that. He thinks on his feet.

'Would it be all right,' I asked, 'if I went to stay with my aunt in Worcestershire?'

He weighed the question, scratching his nose with his stethoscope. He had been doing this at intervals during our get-together, being evidently one of the scratchers, like Barbara Frietchie. The poet Nash would have taken to him.

'I see no objection to your staying with your aunt, provided the conditions are right. Whereabouts in Worcestershire does she live?'

'Near a town called Market Snodsbury.'

'Is the air pure there?'

'Excursion trains are run for people to breathe it.'

'Your life would be quiet?'

'Practically unconscious.'

'No late hours?'

'None. The early dinner, the restful spell with a good book or the crossword puzzle and so to bed.'

'Then by all means do as you suggest.'

'Splendid. I'll ring her up right away.'

The aunt to whom I alluded was my good and deserving

Aunt Dahlia, not to be confused with my Aunt Agatha who eats broken bottles and is strongly suspected of turning into a werewolf at the time of the full moon. Aunt Dahlia is as good a sort as ever said 'Tally Ho' to a fox, which she frequently did in her younger days when out with the Quorn or Pytchley. If she ever turned into a werewolf, it would be one of those jolly breezy werewolves whom it is a pleasure to know.

It was very satisfactory that he had given me the green light without probing further, for an extended quiz might have revealed that Aunt Dahlia has a French cook who defies competition, and I need scarcely explain that the first thing a doctor does when you tell him you are going to a house where there's a French cook is to put you on a diet.

'Then that's that,' I said, all buck and joviality. 'Many thanks for your sympathetic co-operation. Lovely weather we are having, are we not? Good morning, good morning, good morning.'

And I slipped him a purse of gold and went off to phone Aunt Dahlia. I had given up all idea of driving to Brighton for lunch. I had stern work before me – viz. cadging an invitation from this aunt, sometimes a tricky task. In her darker moods, when some domestic upheaval is troubling her, she has been known to ask me if I have a home of my own and, if I have, why the hell I don't stay in it.

I got her after the delays inseparable from telephoning a remote hamlet like Market Snodsbury, where the operators are recruited exclusively from the Worcestershire branch of the Jukes family.

'Hullo, aged relative,' I began, as suavely as I could manage.

'Hullo to you, you young blot on Western civilization,' she responded in the ringing tones with which she had once rebuked hounds for taking time off to chase rabbits. 'What's on your mind, if any? Talk quick, because I'm packing.'

I didn't like the sound of this.

'Packing?' I said. 'Are you going somewhere?'

'Yes, to Somerset, to stay with friends of mine, the Briscoes.'

'Oh, curses.'

'Why?'

'I was hoping I might come to you for a short visit.'

'Well, sucks to you, young Bertie, you can't. Unless you'd like to rally round and keep Tom company.'

I h'm-ed at this. I am very fond of Uncle Tom, but the idea of being cooped up alone with him in his cabin didn't appeal to me. He collects old silver and is apt to hold you with a glittering eye and talk your head off about sconces and foliations and gadroon borders, and my interest in these is what you might call tepid. 'No,' I said. 'Thanks for the kind invitation, but I think I'll take a cottage somewhere.'

Her next words showed that she had failed to grasp the gist.

'What is all this?' she queried. 'I don't get it. Why have you got to go anywhere? Are you on the run from the police?'

'Doctor's orders.'

'What are you talking about? You've always been as fit as ten fiddles.'

'Until this morning, when spots appeared on my chest.'

'Spots?'

'Pink.'

'Probably leprosy.'

'The doc thinks not. His view is that they are caused by my being a typical young man about town who doesn't go to bed early enough. He says I must leg it to the country and breathe pure air, so I shall need a cottage.'

'With honeysuckle climbing over the door and old Mister Moon peeping in through the window?'

'That sort of thing. Any idea how one sets about getting a cottage of that description?'

'I'll find you one. Jimmy Briscoe has dozens. And Maiden Eggesford, where he lives, is not far from the popular seaside resort of Bridmouth-on-Sea, notorious for its invigorating air. Corpses at Bridmouth-on-Sea leap from their biers and dance round the maypole.'

'Sounds good.'

'I'll drop you a line when I've got the cottage. You'll like Maiden Eggesford. Jimmy has a racing stable, and there's a big meeting coming on soon at Bridmouth; so you'll have not only pure air but entertainment. One of Jimmy's horses is running, and most of the wise money is on it, though there is a school of thought that maintains that danger is to be expected from a horse belonging to a Mr Cook. And now for heaven's sake get off the wire. I'm busy.'

So far, I said to myself as I put back the receiver, so g. I would have preferred, of course, to be going to the aged relative's home, where Anatole her superb chef dished up his mouth-waterers, but we Woosters can rough it, and life in a country cottage with the aged r. just around the corner would be a very different thing from a country c. without her to come through with conversation calculated to instruct, elevate and amuse.

All that remained now was to break the news to Jeeves, and I rather shrank from the prospect.

You see, we had practically settled on a visit to New York,

and I knew he was looking forward to it. I don't know what he does in New York, but whatever it is it's something he gets a big kick out of, and disappointment, I feared, would be inevitable.

'Jeeves,' I said when I had returned to the Wooster GHQ, 'I'm afraid I have bad news.'

'Indeed, sir? I am sorry to hear that.'

One of his eyebrows had risen about an eighth of an inch, and I knew he was deeply stirred, because I had rarely seen him raise an eyebrow more than a sixteenth of an inch. He had, of course, leaped to the conclusion that I was about to tell him that the medicine man had given me three months to live, or possibly two. 'Mr Murgatroyd's diagnosis was not encouraging?'

I hastened to relieve his apprehensions.

'Yes, as a matter of fact it was. Most encouraging. He said the spots *qua* spots . . . Is it *qua*?'

'Perfectly correct, sir.'

'His verdict was that the spots *qua* spots didn't amount to a row of beans and could be disregarded. They will pass by me like the idle wind which I respect not.'

'Extremely gratifying, sir.'

'Extremely, as you say. But pause before you go out and dance in the streets, because there's more to come. It was to this that I was alluding when I said I had bad news. I've got to withdraw to the country and lead a quiet life. He says if I don't, he cannot answer for the consequences. So I'm afraid New York is off.'

It must have been a severe blow, but he bore it with the easy nonchalance of a Red Indian at the stake. Not a cry escaped him, merely an 'Indeed, sir?', and I tried to point out the bright side.

'It's a disappointment for you, but it's probably an excellent thing. Everybody in New York is getting mugged these days or shot by youths, and being mugged and shot by youths doesn't do a fellow any good. We shall avoid all that sort of thing at Maiden Eggesford.'

'Sir?'

'Down in Somerset. Aunt Dahlia is visiting friends there and is going to get me a cottage. It's near Bridmouth-on-Sea. Have you ever been to Bridmouth?'

'Frequently, sir, in my boyhood, and I know Maiden Eggesford well. An aunt of mine lives there.'

'And an aunt of mine is going there. What a coincidence.'

I spoke blithely, for this obviously made everything hotsy-totsy. He had probably been looking on beetling off to the country as going into the wilderness, and the ecstasy of finding that the first thing he would set eyes on would be a loved aunt must have been terrific.

So that was that. And having got the bad news broken, I felt at liberty to turn the conversation to other topics, and I thought he would be interested in hearing about my encounter with Plank.

'I got a shock at the doc's, Jeeves.'

'Indeed, sir?'

'Do you remember Major Plank?'

'The name seems vaguely familiar, sir, but only vaguely.'

'Throw the mind back. The explorer bloke who accused me of trying to chisel him out of five quid and was going to call the police, and you came along and said you were Inspector Witherspoon of Scotland Yard and that I was a notorious crook whom you had been after for ages, and I was known as Alpine Joe because I always wore an Alpine hat. And you took me away.'

'Ah, yes, sir, I remember now.'

'I ran into him this morning. He remembered my face, but nothing more except that he said he knew my name began with Al.'

'A most unnerving experience, sir.'

'Yes, it rattled me more than somewhat. It's a great relief to think that I shall never see him again.'

'I can readily understand your feelings, sir.'

In due course Aunt Dahlia rang to say that she had got a cottage for me and to let her know what day I would be arriving.

And so began what I suppose my biographers will refer to as The Maiden Eggesford Horror – or possibly The Curious Case Of The Cat Which Kept Popping Up When Least Expected.

CHAPTER FOUR

I left for Maiden Eggesford a couple of days later in the old two-seater. Jeeves had gone on ahead with the luggage and would be there to greet me on my arrival, no doubt all braced and refreshed from communing with his aunt.

It was in jocund mood that I set forth. There were rather more astigmatic loonies sharing the road with me than I could have wished, but that did nothing to diminish my euphoria, as I have heard it called. The weather couldn't have been better, blue skies and sunshine all over the place, and to put the frosting on the cake E. Jimpson Murgatroyd had been one hundred per cent right about the spots. They had completely disappeared, leaving not a wrack behind, and the skin on my chest was back to its normal alabaster.

I reached journey's end at about the hour of the evening cocktail and got my first glimpse of the rural haven which was to be the Wooster home for I didn't know how long.

Well, I had had a sort of idea that there would be what they call subtle but well-marked differences between Maiden Eggesford and such resorts as Paris and Monte Carlo, and a glance told me I had not erred. It was one of those villages where there isn't much to do except walk down the main street and look at the Jubilee watering-trough and then walk up the main street and look at the Jubilee watering-trough from the other side. E. Jimpson Murgatroyd would have been all for it. 'Oh, boy,' I could hear him saying, 'this is the stuff to give the typical young man about town.' The air, as far as I could tell from the first few puffs, seemed about as pure as could be expected, and I looked forward to a healthy and invigorating stay.

The only thing wrong with the place was that it appeared to be haunted, for as I alighted from the car I distinctly saw the phantasm or wraith of Major Plank. It was coming out of the local inn, the Goose and Grasshopper, and as I gazed at it with bulging eyes it vanished round a corner, leaving me, I need scarcely say, in something of a twitter. I am not, as I mentioned earlier, a fussy man, but nobody likes to have spectres horsing around, and for a while my jocund mood became a bit blue about the edges.

I speedily pulled myself together. 'Twas but a momentary illusion, I said to myself. I reasoned the thing out. If Plank had come to a sticky end since I had seen him last and had started on a haunting career, I said to myself, why should he be haunting Maiden Eggesford when the whole of equatorial Africa was open to him? He would be much happier scaring the daylights out of natives whom he had cause to dislike – the widows and surviving relatives of the late chief of the 'Mgombis, for instance.

Fortified by these reflections, I went into the cottage.

A glance told me it was all right. I think it must have been built for an artist or somebody like that, for it had all the modern cons including electric light and the telephone, being in fact more a desirable bijou residence than a cottage.

Jeeves was there, and he brought me a much-needed refresher – in deference to E. Jimpson Murgatroyd a dry ginger ale. Sipping it, I decided to confide in him, for in spite of the clarity with which I had reasoned with myself I was still not altogether convinced that what I had seen had not been a phantom. True, it had looked solid enough, but I believe the best ghosts often do.

'Most extraordinary thing, Jeeves,' I said, 'I could have sworn I saw Major Plank coming out of the pub just now.'

'No doubt you did, sir. Major Plank would be quite likely to come to the village. He is the guest of Mr Cook of Eggesford Court.'

You could have knocked me down with a cheese straw.

'You mean he's *here*?'

'Yes, sir.'

I was astounded. When he had told me he was off to the country, I had naturally assumed that he meant he was returning to his home in Gloucestershire. Not, of course, that there's any reason why someone who lives in Gloucestershire shouldn't visit Somerset. Aunt Dahlia lives in Worcestershire, and she was visiting Somerset. You have to look at these things from every angle.

Nevertheless, I was perturbed.

'I'm not sure I like this, Jeeves.'

'No, sir?'

'He may remember what our last meeting was all about.'

'It should not be difficult to avoid him, sir.'

'Something in that. Still, what you say has given me a shock. Plank is the last person I want in my neighbourhood. I think, as my nervous system has rather taken the knock, we might discard this ginger ale and substitute for it a dry martini.'

'Very good, sir.'

'Murgatroyd will never know.'

'Precisely, sir.'

And so, having breathed considerable quantities of pure air and taken a couple of refreshing looks at the Jubilee watering-trough, to bed early, as recommended by E. Jimpson Murgatroyd.

The result of this following of doctor's orders was sensational. Say what you might about his whiskers and his habit of looking as if he had been attending the funeral of a dear friend, E. Jimpson knew his job. After about ten hours of restful sleep I sprang from between the sheets, leaped to the bathroom, dressed with a song on my lips and headed for the breakfast table like a two-year-old. I had cleaned up the eggs and b., and got the toast and marmalade down the hatch to the last crumb with all the enthusiasm of a tiger of the jungle tucking into its ration of coolie, and was smoking a soothing cigarette, when the telephone rang and Aunt Dahlia's voice came booming over the wire.

'Hullo, old ancestor,' I said, and it was a treat to hear me, so full of ginger and lovingkindness was my diction. 'A very hearty good morning to you, aged relative.'

'You've got here, have you?'

'In person.'

'So you're still alive. The spots didn't turn out to be fatal.'

'They've entirely disappeared,' I assured her. 'Gone with the wind.'

'That's good. I wouldn't have liked introducing a piebald nephew to the Briscoes, and they want you to come to lunch today.'

'Vastly civil of them.'

'Have you a clean collar?'

'Several, with immaculate shirts attached.'

'Don't wear that Drones Club tie.'

'Certainly not,' I agreed. If the Drones Club tie has a fault, it is a little on the loud side and should not be sprung suddenly on nervous people and invalids, and I had no means of knowing if Mrs Briscoe was one of these. 'What time is the binge?'

'One-thirty.'

'Expect me then with my hair in a braid.'

The invitation showed a neighbourly spirit which I applauded, and I said as much to Jeeves.

'They sound good eggs, these Briscoes.'

'I believe they give uniform satisfaction, sir.'

'Aunt Dahlia didn't say where they lived.'

'At Eggesford Hall, sir.'

'How does one get there?'

'One proceeds up the main street of the village to the high road, where one turns to the left. You cannot miss the house. It is large and stands in extensive grounds. It is a walk of about a mile and a half, if you were intending to walk.'

'I think I'd better. Murgatroyd would advise it. You, I take it, in my absence will go and hobnob with your aunt. Have you seen her yet?'

'No, sir. I learn from the lady behind the bar of the Goose and Grasshopper, where I looked in on the night of my arrival, that she has gone to Liverpool for her annual holiday.'

Liverpool, egad! Sometimes one feels that aunts live for pleasure alone.

I made an early start. If these Briscoes were courting my society, I wanted to give them as much of it as possible.

Reaching the high road, where Jeeves had told me to turn to the left, I thought I had better make sure. He had spoken confidently, but it is always well to get a second opinion. And by jove I found that he had goofed. I accosted a passing centenarian – everybody in Maiden Eggesford seemed to be about a hundred and fifty, no doubt owing to the pure air – and asked which way I turned for Eggesford Court, and he said to the right. It just showed how even Jeeves can be mistaken.

On one point, however, he had been correct. A large house, he had said, standing in extensive grounds, and I had been walking what must have been a mile and a half when I came in sight of just such a residence, standing in grounds such as he had described. There were gates opening on a long drive, and I was starting to walk up this, when it occurred to me that I could save time by cutting across country, because the house I could see through the trees was a good deal to the nor'-nor'-east. They make these drives winding so as to impress visitors. Bless my soul, the visitor says, this drive must be three-quarters of a mile long; shows how rich the chap is.

Whether I was singing or not I can't remember – more probably whistling – but be that as it may I made good progress, and I had just come abreast of what looked like stables when there appeared from nowhere a cat.

It was a cat of rather individual appearance, being black in its general colour scheme but with splashes of white about the ribs and also on the tip of its nose. I chirruped and twiddled my fingers, as is my custom on these occasions, and it advanced with its tail up and rubbed its nose against my leg in a manner that indicated clearly that in Bertram Wooster it was convinced that it had found a kindred soul and one of the boys.

Nor had its intuition led it astray. One of the first poems

I ever learned – I don't know who wrote it, probably Shakespeare – ran:

> I love little pussy; her coat is so warm;
> And if I don't hurt her, she'll do me no harm;

and that is how I have been all my life. Ask any cat with whom I have had dealings what sort of a chap I am cat-wise, and it will tell you that I am a thoroughly good egg in whom complete confidence can safely be placed.

Cats who know me well, like Aunt Dahlia's Augustus, will probably allude to my skill at scratching them behind the ear.

I scratched this one behind the ear, and it received the attention with obvious gratification, purring like the rumble of distant thunder. Cordial relations having now been established, I was proceeding to what you might call Phase Two – viz. picking it up in my arms in order to tickle its stomach – when the welkin was split by a stentorian 'Hi'.

There are many ways of saying 'Hi'. In America it is a pleasant form of greeting, often employed as a substitute for 'Good morning'. Two friends meet. One of them says 'Hi, Bill.' The other replies 'Hi, George.' Then Bill says 'Is this hot enough for you?', and George says that what he minds is not the heat but the humidity, and they go on their way.

But this 'Hi' was something very different. I believe the sort of untamed savages Major Plank mixes with do not go into battle shouting 'Hi', but if they did the sound would be just like the uncouth roar which had nearly shattered my eardrums. Turning, I perceived a red-faced little half-portion brandishing a hunting crop I didn't much like the look of. I have never been fond of hunting crops since at an early age I was chased for a mile across difficult country by an uncle armed with one, who had found me smoking one of his cigars. In frosty weather I can still feel the old wounds.

But now I wasn't really perturbed. This, I took it, was the Colonel Briscoe who had asked me to lunch, and though at the moment he had the air of one who would be glad to dissect me with a blunt knife, better conditions would be bound to prevail as soon as I mentioned my name. I mean, you don't ask a fellow to lunch and start assaulting and battering him as soon as he clocks in.

I mentioned it, accordingly, rather surprised by his size, for I had thought they made colonels somewhat larger. Still, I suppose they come in all sizes, like potatoes or, for the matter of that, girls. Vanessa Cook, for instance, was definitely on the substantial side, whereas others who had turned me down from time to time were practically midgets.

'Wooster, Bertram,' I said, tapping my chest.

I had anticipated an instant cooling of the baser passions, possibly a joyful cry and a 'How are you, my dear fellow, how are you?' accompanied by a sunny smile of welcome, but nothing of the sort occurred. He continued to effervesce, his face now a rather pretty purple.

'What are you doing with that cat?' he demanded hoarsely.

I preserved a dignified calm. I didn't like his tone, but then one often doesn't like people's tones.

'Merely passing the time of day,' I replied with a suavity that became me well.

'You were making away with it.'

'Making a what?'

'Stealing it.'

I drew myself up to my full height, and I shouldn't be

surprised if my eyes didn't flash. I have been accused of a good many things in my time, notably by my Aunt Agatha, but never of stealing cats, and the charge gave deep offence to the Wooster pride. Heated words were on the tip of my tongue, but I kept them in status quo, as the expression is. After all, the man was my host.

With an effort to soothe, I said:

'You wrong me, Colonel. I wouldn't dream such a thing.'

'Yes you would, yes you would, yes you would. And don't call me Colonel.'

It was hardly an encouraging start, but I tried again.

'Nice day.'

'Damn the day.'

'Crops coming on nicely?'

'Curse the crops.'

'How's my aunt?'

'How the devil should I know how your aunt is?'

I thought this odd. When you've got an aunt staying with you, you ought to be able to supply enquirers with a bulletin, if only a sketchy one, of her state of health. I began to wonder if the little shrimp I was chatting with wasn't a bit fuzzy in the upper storey. Certainly, as far as the conversation had gone at present, he would have aroused the professional interest of any qualified brain specialist.

But I didn't give up. We Woosters don't. I tried another tack altogether.

'It was awfully kind of you to ask me to lunch,' I said.

I don't say he actually frothed at the mouth. There was no question, however, that my words had displeased him:

'Ask you to lunch? Ask you to *lunch*? I wouldn't ask you to lunch –'

I think he was about to add 'with a ten-foot pole', but at this moment from off-stage there came the sound of a robust tenor voice singing what sounded like the song hit from some equatorial African musical comedy, and the next moment Major Plank appeared, and the scales fell from my eyes. Plank being on the premises meant that this wasn't the Briscoe residence by a damn sight. By losing faith in Jeeves and turning to the right on reaching the high road, instead of to the left as he had told me to, I had come to the wrong house. For an instant I felt like blaming the centenarian, but we Woosters are fairminded and I remembered that I had asked him the way to Eggesford Court, which this joint presumably was, and if you say Court when you mean Hall, there's bound to be confusion.

'Good Lord,' I said, suffused with embarrassment, 'aren't you Colonel Briscoe?'

He didn't deign to answer that one, and Plank started talking.

'Why, hullo, Wooster,' he said. 'Who would ever have thought of seeing you here? I didn't know you knew Cook.'

'Do *you* know him?' said the purple chap, evidently stunned by the idea that I could have a respectable acquaintance.

'Of course I know him. Met him at my place in Gloucestershire, though under what circumstances I've forgotten. It'll come back, but at the moment all I know is that he has changed his name. It used to be something beginning with Al, and now it's Wooster. I suppose the original name was something ghastly which he couldn't stand any longer. I knew a man at the United Explorers who changed his name from Buggins to Westmacote-Trevelyan. I thought it very sensible of him, but it didn't do him much good, poor chap, because he had scarcely got used to signing his IOUs Gilbert Westmacote-Trevelyan when he was torn asunder by a lion. Still, that's the way it goes. How did you come out with the doctor, Wooster? Was it bubonic plague?'

I said No, not bubonic plague, and he said he was glad to hear it, because bubonic plague was no joke, ask anyone.

'You staying in these parts?'

'No, I have a cottage in the village.'

'Pity. You could have come here. Been company for Vanessa. But you'll join us at lunch?' said Plank, who seemed to think that a guest is entitled to issue invitations to his host's house, which any good etiquette book would have told him is not the case.

'I'm sorry,' I said. 'I'm lunching at Eggesford Hall with the Briscoes.'

This caused Cook, who had been silent for some time, probably having trouble with his vocal cords, to snort visibly.

'I knew it! I was right! I knew you were Briscoe's hireling!'

'What are you talking about, Cook?' asked Plank, not abreast.

'Never mind what I'm talking about. I know what I'm talking about. This man is in the pay of Briscoe, and he came here to steal my cat.'

'Why would he steal your cat?'

'You know why he would steal my cat. You know as well as I do that Briscoe stops at nothing. Look at this man. Look at his face. Guilt written all over it. I caught him with the cat in his arms. Hold him there, Plank, while I go and telephone the police.'

And so saying he legged it.

I confess to being a little uneasy when I heard him tell Plank to hold me, because I had had experience of Plank's methods of holding people. I believe I mentioned earlier that at our previous meeting he had proposed to detain me with the assistance of his Zulu knob-kerrie, and he had in his grasp now a stout stick, which, if it wasn't a Zulu knob-kerrie, was unquestionably the next best thing.

Fortunately he was in a friendly mood.

'You mustn't mind Cook, Wooster. He's upset. He's been having a spot of domestic trouble. That's why he asked me to come and stay. He thought I might have advice to offer. He allowed his daughter Vanessa to go to London to study Art at the Slade, if that's the name of the place, and she got in with the wrong crowd, got pinched by the police and so on and so forth, upon which Cook did the heavy father and jerked her home and told her she had got to stay there till she learned a bit of sense. She doesn't like it, poor girl, but I tell her she's lucky not to be in equatorial Africa, because there if a daughter blots her copybook, her father chops her head off and buries her in the back garden. Well, I hate to see you go, Wooster, but I think you had better be off. I don't say Cook will be back with a shotgun, but you never know. I'd leave, if I were you.' His advice struck me as good. I took it.

CHAPTER FIVE

I headed for the cottage, where I had left the car. By the time I got there I should have done three miles of foot-slogging and I proposed to give the leg muscles a bit of time off, and if E. Jimpson Murgatroyd didn't like it, let him eat cake.

I was particularly anxious to get together with Jeeves and hear what he had to say about the strange experience through which I had just passed, as strange an e. as had come my way in what you might call a month of Sundays.

I could make nothing of the attitude Cook had taken up. Plank's theory that his asperity had been due to the fact that Vanessa had got into the wrong crowd in London seemed to me pure apple sauce. I mean, if your daughter picks her social circle unwisely and starts clobbering the police, you don't necessarily accuse the first person you meet of stealing cats. The two things don't go together.

'Jeeves,' I said, reaching the finish line and sinking into an armchair, 'answer what I am about to ask you frankly. You have known me a good time.'

'Yes, sir.'

'You have had every opportunity of studying my psychology.'

'Yes, sir.'

'Well, would you say I was a fellow who stole cats?'

'No, sir.'

His ready response pleased me not a little. No hesitation, no humming and hawing, just 'No, sir'.

'Exactly what I expected you to say. Just what anyone at the Drones or elsewhere would say. And yet cat-stealing is what I have been accused of.'

'Indeed, sir?'

'By a scarlet-faced blighter named Cook.'

And forthwith, if that's the expression, I told him about my strange e., passing lightly over my not having trusted his directions on reaching the high road. He listened attentively, and when I had finished came as near to smiling as he ever does. That is to say, a muscle at the corner of his mouth twitched slightly as if some flying object such as a mosquito had settled there momentarily.

'I think I can explain, sir.'

It seemed incredible. I felt like Doctor Watson hearing Sherlock Holmes talking about the one hundred and forty-seven varieties of tobacco ash and the time it takes parsley to settle in the butter dish.

'This is astounding, Jeeves,' I said. 'Professor Moriarty wouldn't have lasted a minute with you. You really mean the pieces of the jig-saw puzzle have come together and fallen into their place?'

'Yes, sir.'

'You know all?'

'Yes, sir.'

'Amazing!'

'Elementary, sir. I found the habitues of the Goose and Grasshopper a ready source of information.'

'Oh, you asked the boys in the back room?'

'Yes, sir.'

'And what did they tell you?'

'It appears that bad blood exists between Mr Cook and Colonel Briscoe.'

'They don't like each other, you mean?'

'Precisely, sir.'

'I suppose it's often that way in the country. Not much to do except think what a tick your neighbour is.'

'It may be as you say, sir, but in the present case there is more solid ground for hostility, at least on Mr Cook's part. Colonel Briscoe is chairman of the board of magistrates and in that capacity recently imposed a substantial fine on Mr Cook for moving pigs without a permit.'

I nodded intelligently. I could see how this must have rankled. I do not keep pigs myself, but if I did I should strongly resent not being allowed to give them a change of air and scenery without getting permission from a board of magistrates. Are we in Russia?

'Furthermore –'

'Oh, that wasn't all?'

'No, sir. Furthermore, they are rival owners of racehorses, and that provides another source of friction.'

'Why?'

'Sir?'

'I don't see why. Most of the big owners are very chummy. They love one another like brothers.'

'The big owners, yes, sir. It is different with those whose activities are confined to small local meetings. There the rivalry is more personal and acute. In the forthcoming contest at Bridmouth-on-Sea the race, in the opinion of my informants at the Goose and Grasshopper, will be a duel between Colonel Briscoe's Simla and Mr Cook's Potato Chip. All the other entries are negligible. There is consequently no little friction between the two gentlemen as the date of the contest approaches, and it is of vital importance to both of them that nothing shall go wrong with the training of their respective horses. Rigid attention to training is essential.'

Well, he didn't need to tell me that. An old hand like myself knows how vital rigid training is for success on the turf. I have not forgotten the time at Aunt Dahlia's place in Worcestershire when I had a heavy bet on Marlene Cooper, the gardener's niece, in the Girls' Under Fifteen Egg and Spoon race on Village Sports Day, and on the eve of the meeting she broke training, ate pounds of unripe gooseberries, and got abdominal pains which prevented her showing up at the starting post.

'But, Jeeves,' I said, 'while all this is of absorbing interest, what I want to know is why Cook got into such a frenzy about this cat. You ought to have seen his blood pressure. It shot up like a rocket. He couldn't have been more emotional if he had been a big shot in the Foreign Office and I a heavily veiled woman diffusing a strange exotic scent whom he had caught getting away with the Naval Treaty.'

'Fortunately I am in a position to elucidate the mystery, sir. One of the habitués with whom I fraternized at the Goose and Grasshopper chances to be an employee of Mr Cook, and he furnished me with the facts in the case. The cat was a stray which appeared one morning in the stable yard, and Potato Chip took an instant fancy to it. This, I understand, is not unusual with highly bred horses, though more often it is a goat or a sheep which engages their affection.'

This was quite new stuff to me. First I'd ever heard of it.

'Goat?' I said.

'Yes, sir.'

'Or a sheep?'

'Yes, sir.'

'You mean love at first sight?'

'One might so describe it, sir.'

'What asses horses are, Jeeves.'

'Certainly their mentality is open to criticism, sir.'

'Though I suppose if for weeks you've seen nothing but Cook and stable boys, a cat comes as a nice change. I take it that the friendship ripened?'

'Yes, sir. The cat now sleeps nightly in the horse's stall and is there to meet him when he returns from his daily exercise.'

'The welcome guest?'

'Extremely welcome, sir.'

'They've put down the red carpet for it, you might say. Strange. I'd have thought a human vampire bat like Cook would have had a stray cat off the premises with a single kick.'

'Something of that nature did occur, my informant tells me, and the result was disastrous. Potato Chip became listless and refused his food. Then one day the cat returned, and the horse immediately recovered both vivacity and appetite.'

'Golly!'

'Yes, sir, the story surprised me when I heard it.'

I rose. Time was getting on, and I had a vision of the Briscoes with their noses pressed to the drawing-room window, looking out and telling each other that surely their Wooster ought to have shown up by now.

'Well, many thanks, Jeeves,' I said. 'With your customary what-d'you-call-it you have cast light on what might have

49

remained a permanent brain-teaser. But for you I should have passed sleepless nights wondering what on earth Cook thought he was playing at. I now feel kindlier towards him. I still wouldn't care to have to go on a long walking tour with the son of a what-not, and if he ever gets himself put up for the Drones, I shall certainly blackball him, but I can see his point of view. He finds me clutching his cat, learns that I am on pally terms with his deadly rival the Colonel, and naturally assumes that there is dirty work afoot. No wonder he yelled like a soul in torment and brandished his hunting crop. He deserves considerable credit for not having given me six of the best with it.'

'Your broadminded view is to be applauded, sir.'

'One must always strive to put oneself in the other fellow's place and remember . . . remember what?'

'Tout comprendre c'est tout pardonner.'

'Thank you, Jeeves.'

'Not at all, sir.'

'And now Ho for Eggesford Hall.'

If you ask about me in circles which I frequent, you will be told that I am a good mixer who is always glad to shake hands with new faces, and it ought to have been in merry mood that I braked the car at the front door of Eggesford Hall. But it wasn't. Not that there was anything about the new faces on the other side to give me the pip. Colonel Briscoe proved to be a genial host, Mrs B. a genial hostess. There were also present, besides Aunt Dahlia, the Rev. Ambrose Briscoe, the Colonel's brother, and the latter's daughter Angelica, a very personable wench with whom, had I not been so preoccupied, I should probably have fallen in love. In short, as pleasant a bunch as you could wish to meet.

But that was the trouble. I *was* preoccupied. It wasn't so much finding myself practically next door to Vanessa Cook that worried me. It would be pretty difficult for me to go anywhere in England where there wasn't somebody who had turned me down at one time or another. I have run across them in spots as widely separated as Bude, Cornwall, and Sedbergh, Yorks. No, what was occupying the Wooster mind was the thought of Pop Cook and his hunting crop. It was not agreeable to feel that one was on bad terms with a man who might run amok at any moment and who, if he did, would probably make a beeline for Bertram.

The result was that I did not shine at the festive b. The lunch was excellent and the port with which it concluded definitely super, and I tucked in with a zest which would have made E. Jimpson Murgatroyd draw in a sharp breath, but as far as sprightly conversation went I was a total loss, and the suspicion must have crossed the minds of my host and hostess fairly soon in the proceedings that they were entertaining a Trappist monk with a good appetite.

That this had not failed to cross the mind of Aunt Dahlia was made abundantly clear to me when the meal was over and she took me for a tour of what Jeeves had called the extensive grounds. She ticked me off with her habitual non-mincing of words. All through my life she has been my best friend and severest critic, and when she rebukes a nephew she rebukes him good.

She spoke as follows, her manner and diction similar to those of a sergeant-major addressing recruits.

'What's the matter with you, you poor reptile? I told Jimmy and Elsa that my nephew might look like a half-witted halibut, but wait till he starts talking, I said, he'll have you in stitches.

And what occurs? Quips? Sallies? Diverting anecdotes? No, sir. You sit there stupefying yourself with food, and scarcely a sound out of you except the steady champing of your jaws. I felt like an impresario of performing fleas who has given his star artist a big build-up, only to have him forget his lines on the opening night.'

I bowed my head in shame, knowing how justified was the rebuke. My contribution to what I have heard called the feast of reason and flow of soul had been, as I have indicated, about what you might have expected from a strong silent Englishman with tonsillitis.

'And the way you waded into that port. Like a camel arriving at an oasis after a long journey through desert sands. It was as if you had received private word from Jimmy that he wanted his cellar emptied quick so that he could turn it into a games room. If that's the way you carry on in London, no wonder you come out all over in spots. I'm surprised you can walk.'

She was right. I had to admit it.

'Did you ever see a play called *Ten Nights in a Bar Room?*'

I could bear no more. Weakly I tried to plead my case.

'I am sorry, aged relative. What you say is true. But I am not myself today.'

'Well, that's a bit of luck for everybody.'

'I'm what you could call distraught.'

'You're what I could call a mess.'

'I passed through a strange experience this morning.'

And with no further ado – or is it to-do? I never can remember – I told her my cat-Cook story.

I told it well, and there was no mistaking her interest when I came to the part where Jeeves elucidated the mystery of the cat's importance in the scheme of things.

'Do you mean to say,' she yipped, 'that if you had got away with that cat –'

I had to pull her up here with a touch of austerity. In spite of the clearness with which I had been at pains to tell the story just right she seemed to have got the wrong angle on the thing.

'There was no question, old ancestor, of my getting away with the cat. I was merely doing the civil thing by tickling its stomach.'

'But do you really mean that if someone were to get away with it, it would be all up with Potato Chip's training?'

'So Jeeves informs me, and he had it from a reliable source at the Goose and Grasshopper.'

'H'm.'

'Why do you say H'm?'

'Ha.'

'Why do you say Ha?'

'Never mind.'

But I did mind. When an aunt says 'H'm' and 'Ha', it means something, and I was filled with a nameless fear.

However, I had no time to go into it, for at this moment we were joined by the Rev. Briscoe and his daughter. And shortly afterwards I left.

CHAPTER SIX

The afternoon had now hotted up to quite a marked extent, and what with a substantial lunch and several beakers of port I was more or less in the condition a python gets into after its mid-day meal. A certain drowsiness had stolen over me, so much so that twice in the course of my narrative the aged r. had felt compelled to notify me that if I didn't stop yawning in her face, she would let me have one on the side of my fat head with the parasol with which she was shielding herself from the rays of the sun.

There had been no diminution of this drowsiness since last heard of, and as I bowled along the high road I was practically in dreamland, and it occurred to me that if I didn't pause somewhere and sleep it off, I should shortly become a menace to pedestrians and traffic. The last thing I wanted was to come before my late host in his magisterial capacity, charged with having struck some citizen amidships while under the influence of his port. Colonel Briscoe's port, I mean, not the citizen's. Embarrassing for both of us, though in a way a compliment to the excellence of his cellar.

The high road, like most high roads, was flanked on either side by fields, some with cows, some without, so, the day being as warm as it was, just dropping anchor over here or over there meant getting as cooked to a crisp as Major Plank would have been, had the widows and surviving relatives of the late chief of the 'Mgombis established connection with him. What I wanted was shade, and by great good fortune I came on a little turning leading to wooded country, just what I needed. I drove into this wooded country, stopped the machinery, and it wasn't long before sleep poured over me in a healing wave, as the expression is.

It started off by being one of those dreamless sleeps, but after a while a nightmare took over. It seemed to me that I was out fishing with E. Jimpson Murgatroyd in what appeared to be tropical waters, and he caught a shark and I was having a look at it, when it suddenly got hold of my arm. This of course gave me a start, and I woke. And as I opened my eyes I saw that there was something attached to my port-side biceps, but it wasn't a shark, it was Orlo Porter.

'I beg your pardon, sir,' he was saying, 'for interrupting your doze, but I am a bird-watcher. I was watching a Clarkson's warbler in that thicket over there, and I was afraid your snoring might frighten it away, so might I beg you to go easy on the sound effects. Clarkson's warblers are very sensitive to loud noises, and you were making yourself audible a mile off.'

Or words to that general import.

I would have replied 'Oh, hullo', or something like that, but I was too astonished to speak, partly because I had never suspected that Orlo Porter could be so polite, but principally because he was there at all. I had looked on Maiden Eggesford as somewhere where I would be free from all human society, a haven where I would have peace perfect peace with loved ones far away, as the hymnbook says, and it was turning out to be a sort of meeting place of the nations. First Plank, then Vanessa Cook, and now Orlo Porter. If this sort of thing was going to go on, I told myself, I wouldn't be surprised to see my Aunt Agatha come round the corner arm in arm with E. J. Murgatroyd.

Orlo Porter seemed now to recognize me, for he started like a native of India who sees a scorpion in his path, and went on to say:

'Wooster, you blasted slimy creeping crawling serpent, I might have expected this!'

It was plain that he was not glad to see me, for there was nothing affectionate in what he said or the way he said it, but apart from that I was unable to follow him. He had me at a loss.

'Expected what?' I asked, hoping for footnotes.

'That you would have followed Vanessa here, your object to steal her from me.'

This struck me as so absurd that I laughed a light laugh, and he asked me to stop cackling like a hen whose union had been blest – or laying a blasted egg, as he preferred to put it.

'I haven't followed anyone anywhere,' I said, trying to pour oil on the troubled w.'s. I debated with myself whether to add 'old man', and decided not. I doubt if it would have had much effect, anyway.

'Then why are you here?' he demanded in a voice so fortissimo that it was obvious that he didn't give a damn if Clarkson's warbler heard him and legged it in a panic.

I continued suave.

'The matter is susceptible of a ready explanation,' I said. 'You remember those spots of mine.'

'Don't change the subject.'

'I wasn't. Having inspected the spots, the doc advised me to retire to the country.'

'There are plenty of other places in the country to retire to.'

'Ah,' I said, 'but my Aunt Dahlia is staying with some people here, and I knew it would make all the difference if I had her to exchange ideas with. Very entertaining woman, my Aunt Dahlia. Never a dull moment when she's around.'

This, as I had foreseen, had him stymied. Something of his belligerence left him, and I could see that he was saying to himself, 'Can it be that I have wronged Bertram?' Then he clouded over again.

'All this is very plausible,' he said, 'but it does not explain why you were slinking round Eggesford Court this morning.'

I was amazed. When I was a child, my nurse told me that there was One who was always beside me, spying out all my ways, and that if I refused to eat my spinach I would hear about it on Judgment Day, but it never occurred to me that she was referring to Orlo Porter.

'How on earth do you know that?' I said – or perhaps 'gasped' would be a better word, or even 'gurgled'.

'I was watching the place through my bird-watching binoculars, hoping to get a glimpse of the woman I love.'

This gave me the opportunity to steer the conversation into less controversial topics.

'I had forgotten you were a bird-watcher till you reminded me just now. You went in for it at Oxford, I remember. It isn't a thing I would care to do myself. Not,' I hastened to add, 'that I've anything against bird-watching. Must be most interesting, besides keeping you' – I was about to say 'out of the public houses' but thought it better to change it to 'out in the open air'. 'What's the procedure?' I said. 'I suppose you lurk in a bush till a bird comes along, and then you out with the glasses and watch it.'

I had more to say, notably a question as to who Clarkson was and how he came to have a warbler, but he interrupted me.

'I will tell you why you were sneaking round Eggesford Court this morning. It was in the hope of seeing Vanessa.'

I no-noed, but he paid no attention.

'And I would like to say for your guidance, Wooster, that if I catch you trying to inflict your beastly society on her again, I shall have no hesitation in tearing your insides out.'

He started to walk away, paused, added over his shoulder the words 'With my bare hands' and was gone, whether or not to resume watching Clarkson's warbler, I had no means of knowing. My own feeling was that any level-headed bird with sensitive ears would have removed itself almost immediately after he had begun to speak.

CHAPTER SEVEN

These parting remarks of O. Porter gave me, as may readily be imagined, considerable food for thought. There happened at the moment to be no passers-by, but if any passers had been by, they would have noticed that my brow was knitted and the eyes a bit glazed. This always happens when you are turning things over in your mind and not liking the look of them. You see the same thing in Cabinet ministers when they are asked awkward questions in Parliament.

It was not, of course, the first time an acquaintance had expressed a desire to delve into my interior and remove its contents. Roderick Spode, now going about under the alias of Lord Sidcup, had done so frequently when in the grip of the illusion that I was trying to steal Madeline Bassett from him, little knowing that she gave me a pain in the gizzard and that I would willingly have run a mile in tight shoes to avoid her.

But I had never before had such a sense of imminent peril as now. Spode might talk airily — or is it glibly? — of buttering me over the lawn and jumping on the remains with hobnailed boots, but it was always possible to buoy oneself up with the thought that his bark was worse than his b. I mean to say, a fellow like Spode has a position to keep up. He can't afford to indulge every passing whim. If he goes buttering people over lawns, he's in for trouble. *Debrett's Peerage* tut-tuts, *Burke's Landed Gentry* raises its eyebrows, and as likely as not he gets cut by the County and has to emigrate.

But Orlo Porter was under no such restraint. Being a Communist, he was probably on palsy-walsy terms with half the big shots at the Kremlin, and the more of the bourgeoisie he disembowelled, thé better they would be pleased. 'A young man with the right stuff in him, this Comrade Porter. Got nice ideas,' they would say when reading about the late Wooster. 'We must keep an eye on him with a view to further advancement.'

Obviously, then, the above Porter having expressed himself as he had done about Vanessa Cook, the shrewd thing for me to do was to keep away from her. I put this up to Jeeves when I returned, and he saw eye to eye with me.

'What are those things circumstances have, Jeeves?' I said.

'Sir?'

'You know what I mean. You talk of a something of circumstances which leads to something. Cats enter into it, if I'm not wrong.'

'Would concatenation be the word you are seeking?'

'That's right. It was on the tip of my tongue. Do concatenations of circumstances arise?'

'Yes, sir.'

'Well, one has arisen now. The facts are these. When we were in London, I formed a slight acquaintance with a Miss Cook who turns out to be the daughter of the chap who owns the horse which thinks so highly of that cat. She had a spot of trouble with the police, and her father summoned her home to see that she didn't get into more. So she is now at Eggesford Court. Got the scenario so far?'

'Yes, sir.'

'This caused her betrothed, a man named Porter, to follow her here in order to give her aid and comfort. Got that?'

'Yes, sir. This frequently happens when two young hearts are sundered.'

'Well, I met him this today, and my presence in Maiden Eggesford came as a surprise to him.'

'One can readily imagine it, sir.'

'He took it for granted that I had come in pursuit of Miss Cook.'

'Like young Lochinvar, when he came out of the West.'

The name was new to me, but I didn't ask for further details. I saw that he was following the plot, and it never does, when you're telling a story, to wander off into side issues.

'And he said if I didn't desist, he would tear my insides out with his bare hands.'

'Indeed, sir?'

'You don't know Porter, do you?'

'No, sir.'

'Well, you know Spode. Porter is Spode plus. Hasty temper. Quick to take offence. And the muscles of his brawny arms are strong as iron bands, as the fellow said. The last chap you'd want to annoy. So what do you suggest?'

'I think it would be advisable to avoid the society of Miss Cook.'

'Exactly the idea which occurred to me. And it ought not to be difficult. The chances of Pop Cook asking me to drop in are very slim. So if I take the high road and she takes the low road . . . Answer that, will you, Jeeves,' I said as the telephone rang in the hall. 'It's probably Aunt Dahlia, but it may be Porter, and I do not wish to have speech with him.'

He went out, to return a few moments later.

'It was Miss Cook, sir, speaking from the post office. She desired me to inform you that she would be calling on you immediately.'

A sharp 'Lord-love-a-duck' escaped me, and I eyed him with reproach.

'You didn't think to say I was out?'

'The lady gave me no opportunity of doing so, sir. She delivered her message and rang off without waiting for me to speak.'

My brow got all knitted again.

'This isn't too good, Jeeves.'

'No, sir.'

'Calling at my home address like this.'

'Yes, sir.'

'Who's to say that Orlo Porter is not lurking outside with his bird-watching binoculars?' I said.

But before I could go into the matter in depth, the door bell had rung, and Vanessa Cook was in my midst. Jeeves, I need scarcely say, had vanished like a family spectre at the crack of dawn. He always does when company arrives. I hadn't seen him go, and I doubted if Vanessa had, but he had gone.

As I stood gazing at Vanessa, I was conscious of the uneasiness you feel when you run up against something particularly hot and are wondering when it is going to explode. It was more than a year since I had seen her, except in the distance when about to be scooped in by the police, and the change in her appearance was calculated to curdle the blood a bit. Her outer aspect was still that of a girl who would have drawn whistles from susceptible members of America's armed forces, but there was something sort of formidable about her which had not been there before, something kind of imperious and defiant, if you know what I mean. Due no doubt to the life she had been leading. You can't go heading protest marches and socking the constabulary without it showing.

Hard, that's the word I was trying for. She had always been what they call a proud beauty, but now she was a hard one. Her lips were tightly glued together, her chin protruding, her whole lay-out that of a girl who intended to stand no rannygazoo. Except that the latter was way down in Class D as a looker, while she, as I have indicated, was the pin-up girl to end all pin-up girls, she reminded me of my childhood dancing mistress. The thought occurred to me that in another thirty years or so she would look just like my Aunt Agatha, before whose glare, as is well known, strong men curl up like rabbits.

Nor was there anything in her greeting to put me at my ease. Having given me a nasty look as if I ranked in her esteem in one of the lowest brackets, she said:

'I am very angry with you, Bertie.'

I didn't like the sound of this at all. It is never agreeable to incur the displeasure of a girl with a punch like hers. I said I was sorry to hear that, and asked what seemed to be the trouble.

'Following me here!'

There is nothing that braces one up like being accused of something to which you can find a ready answer. I laughed merrily, and her reaction to my mirth was much the same as Orlo Porter's had been, though where he had spoken of hens laying eggs she preferred the simile of a hyena with a bone stuck in its throat. I said I hadn't had a notion that she was in these parts, and this time she laughed, one of those metallic ones that are no good to man or beast.

'Oh, come!' she said. 'Oddly enough,' she added, 'although I am furious, I can't help admiring you in a way. I am surprised to find that you have so much initiative. It is abominable, but it does show spirit. It makes me feel that if I had married you, I could have made something of you.'

I shuddered from hair-do to shoe-sole. I was even more thankful than before that she had given me the bum's rush. I know what making something of me meant. Ten minutes after the bishop and colleague had done their stuff she would have been starting to mould me and jack up my soul, and I like my soul the way it is. It may not be the sort of soul that gets crowds cheering in the streets, but it suits me and I don't want people fooling about with it.

'But it is quite impossible, Bertie. I love Orlo and can love no one else.'

'That's all right. Entirely up to you. I must put you straight on one thing, though. I really didn't know you were here.'

'Are you trying to make me believe that it was a pure coincidence –'

'No, not that. More what I would call a concatenation of circumstances. My doctor ordered me a quiet life in the country, and I chose Maiden Eggesford because my aunt is staying with some people here and I thought it would be nice being near her. A quiet life in the country can be a bit too quiet if you don't know anybody. She got me this cottage.'

You might have thought that that would have cleaned everything up and made life one grand sweet song, as the fellow said, but no, she went on looking puff-faced. No pleasing some girls.

'So I was wrong in thinking that you had initiative,' she said, and if her lip didn't curl scornfully, I don't know a scornfully curling lip when I see one. 'You are just an ordinary footling member of the bourgeoisie that Orlo dislikes so much.'

'A typical young man about town, some authorities say.'

'I don't suppose you have ever done anything worthwhile in your life.'

I could have made her look pretty silly at this juncture by revealing that I had won a Scripture Knowledge prize at my private school, a handsomely bound copy of a devotional work whose name has escaped me, and that when Aunt Dahlia was running that *Milady's Boudoir* paper of hers I contributed to it an article, or piece as we writers call it, on What The Well-Dressed Man Is Wearing, but I let it go, principally because she had gone on speaking and it is practically impossible to cut in on a woman who has gone on speaking. They get the stuff out so damn quick that the slower male hasn't a hope.

'But the matter of your wasted life is beside the point. God made you, and presumably he knew what he was doing, so we need not go into that. What you will want to hear is my reason for coming to see you.'

'Any time you're passing,' I said in my polished way, but she took no notice and continued.

'Father's friend, Major Plank, who is staying with us, was talking at lunch about someone named Wooster who had called this morning, and when Father turned purple and choked on his lamb cutlet I knew it must be you. You are the sort of young man he dislikes most.'

'Do young men dislike him?'

'Invariably. Father is and always has been a cross between Attila the Hun and a snapping-turtle. Well, having found that you were in Maiden Eggesford I came to ask you to do something for me.'

'Anything I can.'

'It's quite simple. I shall of course be writing to Orlo, but I don't want him to send his letters to the Court because Father, in addition to resembling a snapping-turtle, is a man of low cunning who wouldn't hesitate to intercept and destroy them, and he always gets down to breakfast before I do, which gives him a strategical advantage. By the time I got to the table the cream of my correspondence would be in his trouser pocket. So I am going to tell Orlo to address his letters care of you, and I will call for them every afternoon.'

I never heard a proposition I liked the sound of less. The idea of her calling at the cottage daily, with Orlo Porter, already heated to boiling point, watching its every move, froze my young blood and made my two eyes, like stars, start from their spheres, as I have heard Jeeves put it. It was with infinite relief that I realized a moment later that my fears were groundless, there being no need for correspondence between the parties of the first and second part.

'But he's here,' I said.

'Here? In Maiden Eggesford?'

'Right plump spang in Maiden Eggesford.'

'Are you being funny, Bertie?'

'Of course I'm not being funny. If I were being funny, I'd have had you in convulsions from the outset. I tell you he's here. I met him this afternoon. He was watching a Clarkson's warbler. Arising from which, you don't happen to have any data relating to Clarkson, do you? I've been wondering who he was and how he got a warbler.'

She ignored my observation. This generally happens with me. Show me a woman, I sometimes say, and I will show you someone who is going to ignore my observations.

Looking at her closely, I noted a change in her aspect. I have said that her face had hardened as the result of going about the place socking policemen, but now it had got all soft. And while her two eyes didn't actually start from their spheres, they widened to about the size of regulation golf balls, and a tender smile lit up her map. She said, 'Well, strike me pink!' or words to that effect.

'So he has come! He has followed me!' She spoke as if it had given her no end of a kick that he had done this. Apparently it wasn't being followed that she objected to; it just had to be the right chap. 'Like some knight in shining armour riding up on his white horse.'

Here would have been a chance to give Jeeves's friend who came out of the West a plug by saying that Orlo reminded me of him, but I had to give it a miss because I couldn't remember the fellow's name.

'I wonder how he managed to get away from his job,' I said.

'He was on his annual two weeks' holiday. That is how he came to be at that protest march. He and I were heading the procession.'

'I know. I was watching from afar.'

'I have not found out yet what happened to him that day. After he knocked the policeman down he suddenly disappeared.'

'Always the best thing to do if you knock a policeman down. He jumped into my car and I drove him to safety.'

'Oh, I see.'

I must say I thought she might have put it a bit stronger. One does not desire thanks for these little kindnesses one does here and there, but considering that on his behalf I had interfered with the police in the execution of their duty, if that's how the script reads, thereby rendering myself liable to a sizeable sojourn in chokey, a little enthusiasm would not have been amiss. Nothing to be done about it except give her a reproachful look. I did this. It made no impression whatever, and she proceeded.

'Is he staying at the Goose and Grasshopper?'

'I couldn't say,' I said, and if I spoke with a touch of what-d'you-call-it in my voice, who can blame me? 'When I met him, we talked mostly about my interior organs.'

'What's wrong with your interior organs?'

'Nothing so far, but he thought there might be something later on.'

'He has a wonderfully sympathetic nature.'

'Yes, hasn't he.'

'Did he recommend anything that would be good for you?'

'As a matter of fact he did.'

'How like him!'

She was silent for a while, no doubt pondering on all Orlo's lovable qualities, many of which I had missed. At length she spoke.

'He must be at the Goose and Grasshopper. It's the only decent inn in the place. Go there and tell him to meet me here at three o'clock tomorrow afternoon.'

'Here?'

'Yes.'

'You mean at this cottage?'

'Why not?'

'I thought you might want to see him alone.'

'Oh, that's all right. You can go for a walk.'

Once more I sent up a silent vote of thanks to my guardian angel for having fixed it that this proud beauty should not become Mrs Bertram Wooster. Her cool assumption that she had only got to state her wishes and all and sundry would jump to fulfil them gave me the pip. So stung was the Wooster pride by the thought of being slung out at her bidding from my personal cottage that it is not too much to say that my blood boiled, and I would probably have said something biting like 'Oh, yes?', only I felt that a *preux chevalier*, which I always aim to be, ought not to crush the gentler sex beneath the iron heel, no matter what the provocation.

So I changed it to 'Right-ho', and went off to the Goose and Grasshopper to give Orlo the low-down.

CHAPTER EIGHT

I found him in the private bar having a gin and ginger ale. His face, never much to write home about, was rendered even less of a feast for the eye by a dark scowl. His spirits were plainly at their lowest ebb, as so often happens when Sundered Heart A is feeling that the odds against his clicking with Sundered Heart B cannot be quoted at better than a hundred to eight.

Of course he may have been brooding because he had just heard that a pal of his in Moscow had been liquidated that morning, or he had murdered a capitalist and couldn't think of a way of getting rid of the body, but I preferred to attribute his malaise to frustrated love, and I couldn't help feeling a pang of pity for him.

He looked at me as I entered in a manner which made me realize how little chance there was of our exchanging presents at Christmas, and I remember thinking what a lot of him there was and all of it anti-Wooster. I had often felt the same about Spode. It seemed that there was something about me that aroused the baser passions in men who were eight feet tall and six across. I took this up with Jeeves once, and he agreed that it was singular.

His eye as I approached was what I have heard described as lacklustre. Whatever it was that was causing this V-shaped depression, seeing me had not brought the sunshine into his life. His demeanour was that of any member of a Wednesday matinée audience or, let us say, a dead fish on a fishmonger's slab. Nor did he brighten when I had delivered my message. After I had done so there was a long silence, broken only by the gurgling of ginger ale as it slid down his throat.

Eventually he spoke, his voice rather like that of a living corpse in one of those horror films where the fellow takes the lid off the tomb in the vault beneath the ruined chapel and blowed if the occupant doesn't start a conversation with him.

'I don't understand this.'

'What don't you understand?' I said, adding 'Comrade', for there is never anything lost by being civil. 'Any assistance I can give in the way of solving any little problems you may have will be freely given. I am only here to help.'

The amount of sunny charm I had put into these words ought to have melted the reserve of a brass monkey, but they got absolutely nowhere with him. He continued to eye me in an Aunt Agathaesque manner.

'It seems odd, if as you say you are the merest acquaintance, that she should be paying you clandestine visits at your cottage. Taken in conjunction with your surreptitious appearance at Eggesford Court, it cannot but invite suspicion.'

When someone talks like that, using words like 'clandestine' and 'surreptitious' and saying that something cannot but invite suspicion, the prudent man watches his step. It was a great relief to me that I had a watertight explanation. I gave it with a winning frankness which I felt could scarcely fail to bring home the bacon.

'My appearance at Eggesford Court wasn't surreptitious. I was there because I had come to the wrong house. And Miss Cook's visit to my cottage had to be clandestine because her father watches her as closely as the paper on the wall. And she visited my cottage because there was no other way of getting in touch with you. She didn't know you were in Maiden Eggesford, and she thought if you wrote her a letter that Pop would intercept it, he being a man who would intercept a daughter's letter at the drop of a hat.'

It sounded absolutely copper-bottomed to me, but he went on giving me the eye.

'All the same,' he said, 'I find it curious that she should have confided in you. It suggests an intimacy.'

'Oh, I wouldn't call it that. Girls I hardly know confide in me. They look upon me as a father figure.'

'Father figure my foot. Any girl who takes you for a father figure ought to have her head examined.'

'Well, let us say a brother figure. They know their secrets are safe with good old Bertie.'

'I'm not so sure you are good old Bertie. More like a snake who goes about the place robbing men of the women they love, if you ask me.'

'Certainly not,' I protested, learning for the first time that this was what snakes did.

'Well, it looks fishy to me,' he said. Then to my relief he changed the subject. 'Do you know a man named Spofforth?'

I said No, I didn't think so.

'P. B. Spofforth. Big fellow with a clipped moustache.'

'No, I've never met him.'

'And you won't for some time. He's in hospital.'

'Too bad. What sent him there?'

'I did. He kissed the woman I love at the annual picnic of the Slade Social and Outing Club. Have you ever kissed the woman I love, Wooster?'

'Good Lord, no.'

'Be careful not to. Did she make a long stay at your cottage?'

'No, very short. In and out like a flash, Just had time to say you were like a knight in shining armour riding up on a white horse and to tell me to tell you to show up at my address tomorrow at three on the dot, and she was off.'

This seemed to soothe him. He went on brooding but now not so much like Jack the Ripper getting up steam for his next murder. He was not, however, quite satisfied.

'I don't call it much of an idea meeting at your cottage,' he said.

'Why not?'

'We shall have you underfoot all the time.'

'Oh, that's all right, Comrade. I shall be going for a walk.'

'Ah,' he said, brightening visibly. 'Going for a walk, eh? Just the thing to do. Capital exercise. Bring the roses to your cheeks. Take your time. Don't hurry back. They tell me there are beauty spots around here well worth seeing.'

And on this cordial note we parted, he to go to the bar for another gin and ginger, I to go back and tell Vanessa that the *pourparlers* had been completed and that he would be at the starting post at three pip-emma on the morrow.

'How did he look?' she asked, all eagerness.

It was a little difficult to answer this, because he had looked like a small-time gangster with a painful gum-boil, but I threw together a tactful word or two which, as Jeeves would say, gave satisfaction, and she buzzed off.

Jeeves came shimmering in shortly after she had left. He seemed a shade perturbed.

'We were interrupted in our recent conversation, sir.'

'We were, Jeeves, and I am glad to say that I no longer need your advice. During your absence the situation has become clarified. A meeting has been arranged and will shortly take place, in fact here at this cottage at three o'clock tomorrow afternoon. I, not wishing to intrude, shall be going for a walk.'

'Extremely gratifying, sir,' he said, and I agreed with him that he had *tetigisti*-ed the *rem acu*.

CHAPTER NINE

At five minutes to three on the following afternoon I had girded my loins and was preparing to iris out, when Vanessa Cook arrived. The sight of me appeared to displease her. She frowned as if I were something that didn't smell just right, and said:

'Haven't you gone yet?'

I considered this a shade brusque, even for a proud beauty, but, true to my resolve to be *preux*, I responded suavely:

'Just going.'

'Well, go,' she said, and I went.

The street outside was as usual, offering little entertainment to the sightseer. A few centenarians were dotted about, exchanging reminiscences of the Boer War, and the eye detected a dog which had interested itself in something it had found in the gutter, but otherwise it was empty. I walked down it and had a look at the Jubilee watering-trough and was walking back on the other side, thinking how pleased E. J. Murgatroyd would be if he could see me, when I caught sight of the shop which acted as a post office and remembered that Jeeves had told me that in addition to selling stamps, picture postcards, socks, boots, overalls, pink sweets, yellow sweets, string, cigarettes and stationery it ran a small lending library.

I went in. I had come away rather short of reading matter, and it never does to neglect one's intellectual side.

Like all village lending libraries, this one had not bothered much about keeping itself up to date, and I was hesitating between *By Order Of The Czar* and *The Mystery Of A Hansom Cab*, which seemed the best bets, when the door opened to Angelica Briscoe, the personable wench I had met at lunch. The vicar's daughter, if you remember.

Her behaviour on seeing me was peculiar. She suddenly became all conspiratorial, as if she had been a Nihilist in *By Order Of The Czar* meeting another Nihilist. I had not yet read that opus, but I assumed that it was full of Nihilists who were always meeting other Nihilists and plotting dark plots with them. She clutched my arm and lowering her voice to a sinister whisper said:

'Has he brought it yet?'

I missed her drift by a wide margin. I like to think of myself as a polished man of the world who can kid back and forth with a pretty girl as well as the next chap, but I must confess that my only response to this query was a silent goggle. It struck me as unusual that a vicar's daughter should be a member of a secret society, but I could think of no other explanation for her words. They had sounded like a secret code, the sort of thing you haven't a hope of making sense of if you aren't a unit of The Uncanny Seven in good standing with all your dues paid up.

Eventually I found speech. Not much of it, but some.

'Eh?' I said.

She seemed to feel that her question had been answered.

Her manner changed completely. She dropped the *By Order Of The Czar* stuff and became the nice girl who in all probability played the organ in her father's church.

'I see he hasn't. But of course one has to give him time for a job like that.'

'Like what?'

'I can't explain. Here's Father.'

And the Reverend Briscoe ambled in, his purpose, as it appeared immediately, to purchase half a pound of the pink sweets and half a pound of the yellow as a present for the more deserving of his choir boys. His presence choked the personable wench off from further revelations, and the only conversation that followed had to do with the weather, the condition of the church roof and how-well-your-aunt-is looking-it-was-such-a-pleasure-seeing-her-again. And after a few desultory exchanges I left them and resumed my walk.

It is always difficult to estimate the time two sundered hearts, unexpectedly reunited, will require for picking up the threads. To be on the safe side I gave Orlo and Vanessa about an hour and a half, and when I returned to the cottage I found I had called my shots correctly. Both had legged it.

I was still much perplexed by that utterance of Angelica Briscoe's. The more I brooded on it, the more cryptic, if that's the word, it became. 'Has he brought it yet?', I mean to say. Has who? Brought what? I called Jeeves in, to see what he made of it.

'Tell me, Jeeves,' I said. 'Suppose you were in a shop taking *By Order Of The Czar* out of the lending library and a clergyman's daughter came in and without so much as a preliminary "Hullo, there", said to you, "Has he brought it yet?", what interpretation would you place on those words?'

He pondered, this way and that dividing the swift mind, as I have heard him put it.

'"Has he brought it yet", sir?'

'Just that.'

'I should reach the conclusion that the lady was expecting a male acquaintance to have arrived or to be arriving shortly bearing some unidentified object.'

'Exactly what I thought. What unidentified object we shall presumably learn in God's good time.'

'No doubt, sir.'

'We must wait patiently till all is revealed.'

'Yes, sir.'

'In the meantime, pigeon-holing that for the moment, did Miss Cook and Mr Porter have their conference all right?'

'Yes, sir, they conversed for some time.'

'In low, throbbing voices?'

'No, sir, the voices of both lady and gentleman became noticeably raised.'

'Odd. I thought lovers generally whispered.'

'Not when an argument is in progress, sir.'

'Good Lord. Did they have an argument?'

'A somewhat acrimonious one, sir, plainly audible in the kitchen, where I was reading the volume of Spinoza which you so kindly gave me for Christmas. The door happened to be ajar.'

'So you were an earwitness?'

'Throughout, sir.'

'Tell me all, Jeeves.'

'Very good, sir. I must begin by explaining that Mr Cook is trustee for a sum of money left to Mr Porter by his late uncle, who appears to have been a partner of Mr Cook in various commercial enterprises.'

'Yes, I know about that. Porter told me.'

'Until Mr Cook releases this money Mr Porter is in no position to marry. I gathered that his present occupation is not generously paid.'

'He's an insurance salesman. Didn't I tell you that I had taken out an accident policy with him?'

'Not that I recall, sir.'

'And a life policy as well, both for sums beyond the dreams of avarice. He talked me into it. But I mustn't interrupt you. Go on telling me all.'

'Very good, sir. Miss Cook was urging Mr Porter to demand an interview with her father.'

'In order to make him cough up?'

'Precisely, sir. "Be firm", I heard her say. "Throw your weight about. Look him in the eye and thump the table."'

'She specified that?'

'Yes, sir.'

'To which he replied?'

'That any time he started thumping tables in the presence of Mr Cook you could certify him as mentally unbalanced and ship him off to the nearest home for the insane – or loony-bin, as he phrased it.'

'Strange.'

'Sir?'

'I wouldn't have thought Porter would have shown such what-is-it.'

'Would pusillanimity be the word for which you are groping, sir?'

'Quite possibly. I know it begins with pu. I said it was strange because I hadn't supposed these knights in shining armour were afraid of anything.'

'Apparently they make an exception in the case of Mr Cook. I gathered from your account of your visit to Eggesford Court that he is a gentleman of somewhat formidable personality.'

'You gathered right. Ever hear of Captain Bligh of the Bounty?'

'Yes, sir. I read the book.'

'I saw the movie. Ever hear of Jack the Ripper?'

'Yes, sir.'

'Put them together and what have you got? Cook. It's that hunting crop of his chiefly. You can face a man with fortitude if he has simply got the disposition of a dyspeptic rattlesnake and confines himself to coarse abuse, but put a hunting crop in his hand and that spells trouble. It was a miracle that I escaped from Eggesford Court with my trouser seat unscathed. But go on, Jeeves. What happened then?'

'May I marshal my thoughts, sir?'

'Certainly. Marshal them all you want.'

'Thank you, sir. One aims at coherence.'

Marshalling his thoughts took between twenty and thirty seconds. At the end of that period he resumed his blow-by-blow report of the dust-up between Vanessa Cook and O. J. Porter, which was beginning to look like the biggest thing that had happened since Gene Tunney and Jack Dempsey had their dispute at Chicago.

'It was almost immediately after Mr Porter's refusal to go to Mr Cook and thump tables that Miss Cook introduced the cat into the conversation.'

'Cat? What cat?'

'The one you met at Eggesford Court, with which the horse Potato Chip formed such a durable friendship. Miss Cook was urging Mr Porter to purloin it.'

'Golly!'

'Yes, sir. The female of the species is more deadly than the male.'

Neatly put, I thought.

'Your own?' I said.

'No, sir. A quotation.'

'Well, carry on,' I said, thinking what a lot of good things Shakespeare had said in his time. Female of species deadlier than male. You had only to think of my Aunt Agatha and spouse to realize the truth of this. 'I get the idea, Jeeves. Porter, in possession of the cat, would have a bargaining point with Cook when it came to discussing trust funds.'

'Precisely, sir. *Rem acu tetigisti.*'

'So I take it that he is now at Eggesford Court putting the bite on old Captain Bligh.'

'No, sir. His refusal to do as Miss Cook asked was unequivocal. "Not in a million years" was the expression he used.'

'Not a very co-operative bloke, this O. J. Porter.'

'No, sir.'

'A bit like Balaam's ass,' I said, referring to one of the dramatis personae who had figured in the examination paper the time I won the Scripture Knowledge prize at my private school. 'If you recall, it too dug in its feet and refused to play ball.'

'Yes, sir.'

'That must have made Miss Cook as sore as a sunburned neck.'

'I did gather from her remarks that she was displeased. She accused Mr Porter of being a lily-livered poltroon, and said that she never wished to speak to him again or hear from him by letter, telegram or carrier pigeon.'

'Pretty final.'

'Yes, sir.'

I didn't actually heave a sigh, but I sort of half-heaved one.

To a man of sensibility there is always something sort of sad about young love coming a stinker on the rocks. Myself, I couldn't imagine anyone wanting to marry Orlo Porter and it would have jarred me to the soles of my socks if I had had to marry Vanessa Cook, but they had unquestionably been all for teaming up, and it seemed a shame that harsh words had come between them and the altar rails.

However, there was this to be said in favour of the rift, that it would do Vanessa all the good in the world to find that she had come up against someone she couldn't say 'Go' to and he goeth, as the fellow said. I mentioned this to Jeeves, and he agreed that there was that aspect to the matter.

'Show her that she isn't Cleopatra or somebody.'

'Very true, sir.'

I would gladly have continued our conversation, but I knew he must be wanting to get back to his Spinoza. No doubt I had interrupted him just as Spinoza was on the point of solving the mystery of the headless body on the library floor.

'Right-ho, Jeeves,' I said. 'That'll be all for the moment.'

'Thank you, sir.'

'If any solution of that "Has he brought it yet?" thing occurs to you, send me an inter-office memo.'

I spoke lightly, but I wasn't feeling so dashed light. Those cryptic words of Angelica Briscoe had shaken me. They seemed to suggest that things were going on behind my back which weren't likely to do me any good. I had suffered so much in the past from girls of Angelica's age starting something – Stiffy Byng is a name that springs to the mind – that I have become wary and suspicious, like a fox that had had the Pytchley after it for years.

By speaking in riddles, as the expression is, A. Briscoe had given me a mystery to chew on; and while mysteries are fine in books – I am never happier than when curled up with the latest Agatha Christie – you don't want them in your private life, for that's how you get headaches.

I was beginning to get one now, when my mind was taken off the throbbing which had started. The front door was open, and through it came Vanessa Cook.

She bore traces of the recent set-to. The cheeks were flushed, the eyes glittering, and looking at the teeth one was left in no doubt that they had been well gnashed in the not too distant past. Her whole demeanour was that of a girl whose emotional nature had been stirred up as if a cyclone had hit it.

'Bertie,' she said.

'Hullo?' I said.

'Bertie,' she said, 'I will be your wife.'

You would have expected this to have drawn some comment from me such as 'Oh, my God!' or 'You'll be my *What*?', but I remained *sotto voce* and the silent tomb, my eyes bulging like those of the fellows I've heard Jeeves mention, who looked at each other with a wild surmise, silent upon a peak in Darien.

The thing had come on me as such a complete surprise. Her rejection of my addresses at the time when I proposed to her had been so definite that it had seemed to me that all danger from that quarter had passed and that from now on we wouldn't even be just good friends. Certainly she had given no indication that she would not prefer to be dead in a ditch rather than married to me. And now this. Is any man safe, one asked oneself. No wonder words failed me, as the expression is.

She, on the other hand, became chatty. Getting the thing off her chest seemed to have done her good. The glitter of her eyes was practically switched off, and she was not clenching her teeth any more. I don't say that even now I would have cared to meet her down a dark alley, but there was a distinct general improvement.

'We shall have quite a quiet wedding,' she said. 'Just a few people I know in London. And it may have to be even quieter than that. It all depends on Father. Your standing with him is roughly what that of a Public Enemy Number One would be at the annual Policeman's Ball. What you did to him I don't know, but I have never seen him a brighter mauve than when your name came up at the luncheon table. If he persists in this attitude, we shall have to elope. That will be perfectly all right with me. I suppose many people would say I was being rash, but I am prepared to take the chance. I know very little of you, true, but anyone the mention of whose name can make Father swallow his lunch the wrong way cannot be wholly bad.'

At last managing to free my tongue from the uvula with which it had become entangled, I found speech, as I dare say those Darien fellows did eventually.

'But I don't understand!'

'What don't you understand?'

'I thought you were going to marry Orlo Porter.'

She uttered a sound rather like an elephant taking its foot out of a mud hole in a Burmese teak forest. The name appeared to have touched an exposed nerve.

'You did, did you? You were mistaken. Would any girl with an ounce of sense marry a man who refuses to do the least little thing she asks him because he is afraid of her father? I shall always be glad to see Orlo Porter fall downstairs and break his neck. Nothing would give me greater pleasure than to read his name in *The Times* obituary column. But marry him? What an idea! No, I am quite content with you, Bertie. By the way, I do dislike that name Bertie. I think I shall call you Harold. Yes, I am perfectly satisfied with you. You have many faults, of course. I shall be pointing some of them out when I am at leisure. For one thing,' she said, not waiting till she was at leisure, 'you smoke too much. You must give that up when we are married. Smoking is just a habit. Tolstoy,' she said, mentioning someone I had not met, 'says that just as much pleasure can be got from twirling the fingers.'

My impulse was to tell her Tolstoy was off his onion, but I choked down the heated words. For all I knew, the man might be a bosom pal of hers and she might resent criticism of him, however justified. And one knew what happened to people, policemen for instance, whose criticism she resented.

'And that silly laugh of yours, you must correct that. If you are amused, a quiet smile is ample. Lord Chesterfield said that since he had had the full use of his reason nobody had ever heard him laugh. I don't suppose you have read Lord Chesterfield's *Letters To His Son*?'

... Well, of course I hadn't. Bertram Wooster does not read other people's letters. If I were employed in the post office, I wouldn't even read the postcards.

'I will draft out a whole course of reading for you.'

She would probably have gone on to name a few of the authors she had in mind, but at this moment Angelica Briscoe came bursting in.

'Has he brought it yet?' she yipped.

Then she saw Vanessa, added the word 'Golly', and disappeared like an eel into mud. Vanessa followed her with an indulgent eye.

'Eccentric child,' she said.

I agreed that Angelica Briscoe moved in a mysterious way her wonders to perform, and shortly after Vanessa went off, leaving me to totter to a chair and bury my face in my hands.

I was doing this, and very natural, too, considering that I

had just become engaged to a girl who was going to try to make me stop smoking, when from outside the front door there came the unmistakable sound of an aunt tripping over a door mat. The next moment, my late father's sister Dahlia staggered in, pirouetted awhile, cursed a bit, recovered her equilibrium and said:

'Has he brought it yet?'

I am not, I think, an irascible man, particularly in my dealings with the gentler sex, but when every ruddy female you meet bellows 'Has he brought it yet?' at you, it does something to your aplomb. I gave her a look which I suppose no nephew should have given an aunt, and it was with no little asperity that I said:

'If some of you girls would stop talking as if you were characters in *By Order Of The Czar*, the world would be a better place. Brought what?'

'The cat, of course, you poor dumb-bell,' she responded in the breezy manner which had made her the popular toast of both the Quorn and the Pytchley fox-hunting organizations. 'Cook's cat. I'm kidnapping it. Or, rather, my agent is acting for me. I told him to bring it here.'

I was reft, as they say, of speech. If there is one thing that affects a nephew's vocal cords, it is the discovery that a loved aunt is all foggy about the difference between right and wrong. Experience over the years ought to have taught me that where this aunt was concerned anything went and the sky was the limit, but nevertheless I was . . . I know there's a word that just describes it . . . Ah, yes, I thought I'd get it . . . I was dumbfounded.

Well, of course, what every woman wants when she has a tale to tell is a dumbfounded audience, and it did not surprise me when she took advantage of my silence to carry on. Naturally aware that her goings-on required a bit of explanation, she made quite a production number of it. I won't say that she omitted no detail however slight, but she certainly didn't condense. She started off at 75 m.p.h. thus:

'I must begin by making clear to the meanest intelligence – yours, to take an instance at random – how extremely sticky my position was on coming to stay with the Briscoes. Jimmy, when inviting me to Eggesford Hall, had written in the most enthusiastic terms of his horse Simla's chances in the forthcoming race. He said he was a snip and putting a large bet on him would be like finding money in the street. And I, poor weak woman, allowed myself to be persuaded. I wagered everything I possessed, down to my more intimate garments. It was only after I got here and canvassed local opinion that I realized that Simla was not a snip or anything like a snip. Cook's Potato Chip was just as fast and had just as much staying power. In fact, the thing would probably end in a dead-heat unless, get this, Bertie, unless one of the two animals blew up in its training. And then you came along with your special information about Potato Chip not being able to keep his mind on the race without this cat there to egg him on, and a bright light shone on me. "Out of the mouths of babes and sucklings!" I said to myself. "Out of the mouths of babes and sucklings!"'

I could have wished that she had phrased it differently, but there was no chance of telling her so. When the aged relative collars the conversation, she collars it.

'I was saying,' she proceeded, 'that I wagered on Simla

everything I possessed. Correction. Change that to considerably more than I possessed. If I lost, it would mean touching Tom for a goodish bit before I could brass up, and you know how parting with money always gives him indigestion. You can picture my state of mind. If it hadn't been for Angelica Briscoe, I think I would have had a nervous breakdown. There were moments when only my iron will kept me from shooting up to the ceiling, shrieking like a banshee. The suspense was so terrific.'

I was still dumbfounded, but I managed to say 'Angelica Briscoe?', at a loss to see where she got into the act, and the speaker spoke on.

'Don't tell me you've forgotten her. I would have thought by this time you would have asked her to marry you, which seems to be your normal practice five minutes after you've met any girl who isn't actually repulsive. But I suppose you couldn't see straight after all that port. Angelica, daughter of the Rev. Briscoe. I had a long talk with her after you had left, and I found that she, too, had betted heavily on Simla and was wondering how she could pay up if he lost. I told her about the cat and she was enthusiastically in favour of stealing it, and she solved the problem which had been bothering me, the question of how it could be done. You see, it's not a job that's up everybody's street. Mine, for instance. You have to be like one of those Red Indians I used to read about in Fenimore Cooper's books when I was a child, the fellows who never let a twig snap beneath their feet, and I'm not built for that.'

There was justice in this. I believe the old relative was sylphlike in her youth, but the years have brought with them a certain solidity, and any twig trodden on by her in the evening of her life would go off like the explosion of a gas main.

'But Angelica pointed the way. There's a girl, that Angelica. Only a clergyman's daughter, but with all the executive qualities of a great statesman. She didn't hesitate a moment. Her face lighting up and her eyes sparkling. She said:

'"This is a job for Billy Graham."'

I could not follow her here. The name was familiar to me, but I never associated it with proficiency in the art of removing cats from Spot A to Spot B, especially cats belonging to someone else. Indeed, I should have thought that that was the sort of activity Mr Graham would rather have frowned on, being in his particular line of business.

I mentioned this to the old ancestor, and she told me I had fallen into a natural error.

'His real name is Herbert Graham, but everyone calls him Billy.'

'Why?'

'Rustic humour. There's a lot of that around here. He's the king of the local poachers, and you don't find any twigs snapping beneath *his* feet. All the gamekeepers for miles around have been trying for years to catch him with the goods, but they haven't a hope. It is estimated that seventy-six point eight per cent of the beer sold in the Goose and Grasshopper is bought by haggard gamekeepers trying to drown their sorrows after being baffled by Billy. I have this on the authority of Angelica, who is a great buddy of his. She told him about our anxiety, and he said he would attend to the matter immediately. He is particularly well situated to carry out operations at the Court, as his niece Marlene is the scullery maid there, so it arouses no suspicion if he is caught hanging around. He can always say he has come to see if she's getting on all right. Really, the whole thing has worked out so smoothly that one feels one is being watched over by Providence.'

I went on being appalled. Her scheme of engaging the services of a hired bravo who would probably blackmail her for the rest of her life shook me to the core. As for Angelica Briscoe, one asked oneself what clergymen's daughters were coming to.

I tried to reason with her.

'You can't do this, old blood relation. It's as bad as nobbling a horse.'

If you think that caused the blush of shame to mantle her cheek, you don't know much about aunts.

'Well, isn't nobbling a horse an ordinary business precaution everyone would take if only they could manage it?' she riposted.

The Woosters never give up. I tried again.

'How about the purity of the turf ?'

'No good to me. I like my turf impure. More genuine excitement.'

'What would the Quorn say of this? Or, for the matter of that, the Pytchley?'

'They would send me a telegram wishing me luck. You don't understand these small country meetings. It's not like Epsom or Ascot. A little finesse from time to time is taken for granted. It's expected of you. A couple of years ago Jimmy had a horse called Poonah running at Bridmouth, and a minion of Cook's got hold of the jockey on the eve of the race, lured him into the Goose and Grasshopper and filled him up with strong drink, sending him to the starting post next day with such a hangover that all he wanted to do was sit down and cry. He came in fifth, sobbing bitterly, and went to sleep before he was out of the saddle. Of course Jimmy guessed what had happened, but nothing was ever said about it. No hard feelings on either side. It wasn't till Jimmy fined Cook for moving pigs without a permit that relations became strained.'

I put another point, a shrewd one.

'What happens if this fellow of yours does get caught? His first move will be to give you away, blackening your reputation in Maiden Eggesford beyond repair.'

'He's never caught. He's the local Scarlet Pimpernel. And nothing could blacken my reputation in Maiden Eggesford. I'm much too much the popular pet ever since I sang "Every Nice Girl Loves A Sailor" at the village concert last year. I had them rolling in the aisles. Three encores, and so many bows that I got a crick in the back.'

'Spare me the tale of your excesses,' I said distantly.

'I wore a sailor suit.'

'Please,' I said, revolted.

'And you ought to have seen the notice I got in the *Bridmouth Argus,* with which is incorporated the *Somerset Farmer* and the *South Country Intelligencer.* But I can't stop here all day listening to you. Elsa's got some bores coming to tea and wants me to rally round. Entertain the cat when it arrives. I gather that it is rather the Bohemian type and probably prefers whisky, but try it with a spot of milk.'

And with these words she exited left centre, as full of beans as any aunt that ever stepped.

Jeeves entered. He had his arms full.

'We appear to have this cat, sir,' he said.

I gave him a look, lacklustre to the last drop.

'So he brought it?'

'Yes, sir. A few moments ago.'

'To the back door?'

'Yes, sir. He showed a proper feeling in that.'

'Is he here now?'

'No, sir. He has gone to the Goose and Grasshopper.'

I got down to the *res*. This was no time for beating about the bush. I needed his advice, and I needed it quick.

'I take it, Jeeves,' I said, 'that seeing the cat at this address you have put two and two together, as the expression is, and realize that there has been dirty work at the crossroads?'

'Yes, sir. I had the advantage of hearing Mrs Travers's observations. She is a lady with a very carrying voice.'

'That expresses it to a nicety. I believe that when hunting in her younger days she could make herself heard in several adjoining counties.'

'I can readily credit it, sir.'

'Well, if you know all about it, there's no need to explain the situation. The problem that confronts us now is where do we go from here?'

'Sir?'

'You know what I mean. I can't just sit here . . . what's the word?'

'Supinely, sir?'

'That's it. I can't just sit here supinely and allow the ranny-gazoo to proceed unchecked. The honour of the Woosters is at stake.'

'You are blameless, sir. You did not purloin the cat.'

'No, but a member of my family did. By the way, could she get jugged if the crime were brought home to her?'

'It is difficult to say without consulting a competent legal authority. But an unpleasant scandal would inevitably result.'

'You mean her name would become a hissing and a byword?'

'Substantially that, sir.'

'With disastrous effects on Uncle Tom's digestion. That's bad, Jeeves. We can't have that. You know how he is after the mildest lobster. We must return this cat to Cook.'

'It would seem advisable, sir.'

'You wouldn't care to do it?'

'No, sir.'

'It would be the feudal thing to do.'

'No doubt, sir.'

'One of those vassals in the Middle Ages would have jumped to it.'

'Very possibly, sir.'

'It would take you ten minutes. You could go in the car.'

'I fear that I must continue to plead a *nolle prosequi*, sir.'

'Then I shall have to see what I can do. Leave me, Jeeves, I want to think.'

'Very good, sir. Would a whisky and soda be of assistance?'

'*Rem acu tetigisti*,' I said.

Left alone, I gave my problem the cream of the Wooster brain for some time, but without avail, as they say. Try as I would I couldn't seem to hit on a method of getting the cat back to square one which didn't involve a meeting with Pop Cook and his hunting crop, and I didn't want that whistling about my legs. Courageous though the Woosters are, there are things from which they shrink.

I was still thinking when there was a cheery cry from without and the blood froze in my veins as Plank came bounding in.

CHAPTER TWELVE

The reason why the blood froze in my v. needs little explanation. The dullest eye could have perceived the delicacy of my position. With the cat practically *vis-à-vis* as you might say and Plank among those present, my predicament was that of a member of the criminal classes who has got away with the Maharajah's ruby and after stashing it among his effects sees a high official of Scotland Yard walk in at the door. Worse, as a matter of fact, because rubies don't talk, whereas cats do. This one had struck me during our brief acquaintance as the taciturn type, content merely to purr, but who knew that, finding itself in unfamiliar surroundings and missing its pal Potato Chip, it would not utter a yowl or two? And a single mew would be enough to plunge me in the soup.

I remember my Aunt Agatha once making me take her revolting son, young Thos, to a play at the Old Vic by the name of *Macbeth*. Thos slept throughout, but I thought it rather good and the reason I bring it up is because there was a scene in it where Macbeth is giving a big dinner party and the ghost of a fellow called Banquo, whom he has recently murdered, crashes the gate all covered with blood. Macbeth took it big, and the point I'm trying to make is that my feelings on seeing Plank were much the same as his on that occasion. I goggled at him as he would have goggled at a scorpion or tarantula or whatever they have in Africa if on going to bed one night he had found it nestling in his pyjamas.

Plank was very merry and bright.

'I thought I'd come and tell you,' he said, 'that I'm getting my memory back. Pretty soon I'll be remembering every detail of that first meeting of ours. Wrapped in mist at the moment, but light is beginning to seep through. It's often that way with malaria.'

I didn't like the sound of this at all. As I explained earlier, the meeting to which he referred had been one fraught with embarrassment for me, and I would have preferred to let the dead past bury its dead as the fellow said. Well, when I remind you that it concluded with a suggestion on his part that he hit me over the head with a Zulu knob-kerrie, you will probably gather that it had not been conducted throughout in an atmosphere of the utmost cordiality.

'One thing I remember,' he proceeded, 'is that you were very keen on Rugby football, which of course is the great interest of my life, and I told you my village team was shaping well and showed great promise. And by an extraordinary stroke of luck I've got a new vicar, chap called Pinker, who was an international prop forward. Played for Oxford four years and got I don't know how many English caps. He pulls the whole side together, besides preaching an excellent sermon.'

Nothing could have pleased me more than to hear that my old friend Stinker Pinker was giving satisfaction, and if it had not been for the dark shadow of the cat brooding over us I might quite have enjoyed this little get-together. For he was an entertaining companion, as these far-flung chaps so often are, and told me a lot I hadn't known before about tsetse flies and what to do if cornered by a charging rhinoceros. But in the middle of one of his best stories – he had just got to where the natives seemed friendly, so he decided to stay the night – he broke off, cocked his head sideways, and said:

'What was that?'

I had heard it, too, of course. But I preserved my poise.

'What was what?' I said.

'I heard a cat.'

I continued to wear the mask. I laughed a light laugh.

'Oh, that was my man Jeeves. He imitates cats.'

'He does, eh?'

'It gives him a passing pleasure.'

'And, I suppose, gets a laugh if he does it at the pub near closing time when everyone's fairly tight. I had a native bearer once who could imitate the mating call of the male puma.'

'Really?'

'So that even female pumas were deceived. They used to come flocking round the camp in dozens, and were as sick as mud when they found it was only a native bearer. He was the one I was telling you we had to bury before sundown. Which reminds me. How are those spots of yours?'

'Completely disappeared.'

'Not always a good sign. It's bad if they work inward and get mixed up with the blood stream.'

'Doctor Murgatroyd expected them to disappear.'

'He ought to know.'

'I have great confidence in him.'

'So have I, in spite of those whiskers.' He paused, and laughed amusedly. 'Odd, the passage of time.'

'Pretty odd,' I conceded.

'Old Jimpy Murgatroyd. You'd never think, to look at him now, that when I knew him as a boy he was about the best wing-three we ever had at Haileybury. Fast as a streak and never failed to give the reverse pass. He scored two tries against Bedford, one of them from our twenty-five, and dropped a goal against Tonbridge.'

Though not having a clue to what he was talking about, I said 'Really?' and he said 'Absolutely', and I think we should have had a lot more about E. Jimpson Murgatroyd the boy, but at this moment the cat came on the air again and he changed the subject.

'Listen. Wouldn't you swear that was a cat? That man of yours certainly makes it lifelike.'

'Just a knack.'

'A gift, I'd call it. Good animal-impersonators don't grow on every bush. I never had another bearer like the puma chap. Plenty of fellows who could do you a passable screech owl, but that's not the same thing. It's lucky Cook isn't here.'

'Why do you say that?'

'Because he would insist on being confronted by what he imagined to be his cat and would tear the place apart to get at it. He wouldn't believe for a moment that it was your man practising his art. You see, a very valuable cat belonging to Cook has vanished, and he is convinced that rival interests have stolen it. He talked of calling Scotland Yard in. But I must be getting along. I only stopped by to tell you about the remarkable improvement in my memory. It's all coming back. It won't be long before I shall be remembering why I thought your name was something that began with Al. Could it have been a nickname of some sort?'

'I don't think so.'

'Not short for Alka-Seltzer, or something like that? Well, no good worrying about it now. It'll come. It'll come.'

I couldn't imagine what had given him this idea that my name began with Al, but it was a small point and I didn't linger on it. No sooner had he beetled off than I was calling Jeeves in for a conference.

When he came, he was full of apologies. He seemed to think he had let the young master down.

'I fear you will have thought me remiss, sir, but I found it impossible to stifle the animal's cries completely. I trust they were not overheard by your visitor.'

'They were, and the visitor was none other than Major Plank, from whom you saved me so adroitly at Totleigh-in-the-Wold. He is closely allied to Pop Cook, and I don't mind telling you that when he blew in I was as badly rattled as Macbeth, if you know what I mean, that time he was sitting down to dinner and the ghost turned up.'

'I know the scene well, sir. "Never shake thy gory locks at me," he said.'

'And I don't blame him. Plank heard those yowls.'

'I am extremely sorry, sir.'

'Not your fault. Cats will be cats. I was taken aback at the moment, like Macbeth, but I kept my head. I told him you were a cat-imitator brushing up your cat-imitating.'

'A very ingenious ruse, sir.'

'Yes, I didn't think it was too bad.'

'Did it satisfy the gentleman?'

'It seemed to. But what of Pop Cook?'

'Sir?'

'What's worrying me is the possibility of Cook being less inclined to swallow the story and coming here to search the premises. And when I say the possibility, I mean the certainty. Figure it out for yourself. He finds me up at Eggesford Court apparently swiping the cat. He learns that I am lunching at Eggesford Hall. "Ha!" he says to himself, "one of the Briscoe gang, is he? And I caught him with the cat actually on his person." Do you suppose that when Plank gets back and tells him he heard someone imitating cats *chez* me, he is going to believe that what Plank heard was a human voice? I doubt it, Jeeves. He will be at my door in ten seconds flat, probably accompanied by the entire local police force.'

My remorseless reasoning had its effect. A slight wiggling of the nose showed that. Nothing could ever make Jeeves say 'Gorblimey!', but I could see that was the word that would have sprung to his lips if he hadn't stopped it half-way. His comment on my *obiter dicta* was brief and to the point.

'We must act, sir!'

'And without stopping to pick daisies by the wayside. Are you still resolved not to return this cat to *status quo*?'

'Yes, sir.'

'Sam Weller would have done it like a shot to oblige Mr Pickwick.'

'It is not my place to return cats, sir. But if I might make a suggestion.'

'Speak on, Jeeves.'

'Why should we not place the matter in the hands of the man Graham?'

'Of course! I never thought of that.'

'He is a poacher of established reputation, and a competent poacher is what we need.'

'I see what you mean. His experience enables him to move

around without letting a twig snap beneath his feet, which is the first essential when you are returning cats.'

'Precisely, sir. With your permission I will go to the Goose and Grasshopper and tell him that you wish to see him.'

'Do so, Jeeves,' I said, and only a few minutes later I found myself closeted with Herbert (Billy) Graham.

The first thing that impressed itself on me as I gave him the once-over was his air of respectability. I had always supposed that poachers were tough-looking eggs who wore whatever they could borrow from the nearest scarecrow and shaved only once a week. He, to the contrary, was neatly clad in form-fitting tweeds and was shaven to the bone. His eyes were frank and blue, his hair a becoming grey. I have seen more raffish Cabinet ministers. He looked like someone who might have sung in the sainted Briscoe's church choir, as I was informed later he did, being the possessor of a musical tenor voice which came in handy for the anthem and when they were doing those 'miserable sinner' bits in the Litany.

He was about the height and tonnage of Fred Astaire, and he had the lissomness which is such an asset in his chosen profession. One could readily imagine him flitting silently through the undergrowth with a couple of rabbits in his grasp, always two jumps ahead of the gamekeepers who were trying to locate him. The old ancestor had compared him to the Scarlet Pimpernel, and a glance was enough to tell me that the tribute was well deserved. I thought how wise Jeeves had been in suggesting that I entrust to him the delicate mission which I had in mind. When it comes to returning cats that have been snitched from their lawful homes, you need a specialist. Where Lloyd George or Winston Churchill would have failed, this Graham, I knew would succeed.

'Good afternoon, sir,' he said, 'you wished to see me?'

I got down without delay to the nub. No sense in humming or, for the matter of that, hawing.

'It's about this cat.'

'I delivered it according to instructions.'

'And now I want you to take it back.'

He seemed perplexed.

'Back, sir?'

'To where you got it.'

'I do not quite understand, sir.'

'I'll explain.'

I think I outlined the position of affairs rather well, making it abundantly clear that a Wooster could not countenance what was virtually tantamount, if tantamount is the word I want, to nobbling a horse and that the cat under advisement must be restored to its proprietor with all possible slippiness, and he listened attentively. But when I had finished, he shook his head.

'Out of the question, sir.'

'Out of the question? Why? You purloined it.'

'Yes, sir.'

'Then you can put it back.'

'No, sir. You are overlooking certain vital facts.'

'Such as?'

'The theft to which you refer was perpetrated as a personal favour to Miss Briscoe, whom I have known from childhood, and a sweet child she was.'

I thought of trying to move him by saying that I had been a sweet child, too, but I knew that this was not the case, having frequently been informed to that effect by my Aunt Agatha, so I let it go. There was not much chance, of course, that he had ever met my Aunt Agatha and discussed me with her, but it was not worth risking.

'Furthermore,' he proceeded, and I was impressed, as I had been from the start, by the purity of his diction. He had evidently had a good education, though I doubted if he was an Oxford man. 'Furthermore,' he said, 'I have five pounds on Potato Chip with the landlord of the Goose and Grasshopper.'

'Aha!' I said to myself, and I'll tell you why I said 'Aha' to myself. I said it because the scales had fallen from my eyes and I saw all. Plainly that stuff about personal favours to sweet children had been the merest bobbledy-gook. He had been actuated throughout entirely by commercial motives. When Angelica Briscoe had come to him, he would have started with a regretful *nolle prosequi* on the ground that he had this fiver on Potato Chip and was obliged to protect his investment. She had said, would he do it for ten quid, which would leave him with a nice profit? He had right-hoed. Angelica had then touched Aunt Dahlia for ten and the deal had gone through. I have often thought I would have made a good detective. I can reason and deduce.

Everything was simple now that the matter could be put on a business basis. All that remained was to arrange terms. It would have to be a ready-money transaction, he being the shrewd man he was, and fortunately I had brought wads of cash with me for betting-on-the-course-at-Bridmouth purposes, so there was no problem.

'How much do you want?' I said.

'Sir?'

'To de-cat my premises and restore this feline to the strength.'

A sort of film came over his frank blue eyes, as I suppose it always did when he talked business, though not when singing in the choir. Fellows at the Drones have told me they notice the same thing in Oofy Prosser, the club millionaire, when they try to float a small loan with him to see them through till next Wednesday.

'How much do I want, sir?'

'Yes. Give it a name. We won't haggle.'

He pursed his lips.

'I'm afraid,' he said, having unpursed them, 'I couldn't do it as cheap as I'd like, sir. You see, what with them having discovered the animal's absence by this time, the hue and cry, as you might say, will be up and everybody at Mr Cook's residence on the *qui vive* or alert. I'd be in the position of a spy in wartime carrying secret dispatches through the enemy's lines with every eye on the look-out for him. I'd have to make it twenty pounds.'

I was relieved. I had been expecting something higher. He, too, seemed to feel that he had erred on the side of moderation, for he immediately added:

'Or, rather, thirty.'

'Thirty!'

'Thirty, sir.'

'Let's haggle,' I said.

But when I suggested twenty-five, a nicer-looking sort of number than thirty, he shook his grey head regretfully, so we went on haggling, and he haggled better than me, so that eventually we settled on thirty-five.

It wasn't one of my best haggling days.

CHAPTER THIRTEEN

One of the questions put to me when I won that Scripture Knowledge prize at my private school was, I recall, 'What do you know of the deaf adder?', and my grip on Holy Writ enabled me to reply correctly that it stopped its ears and would not hear the voice of the charmer, charm he never so wisely, and after my session with Herbert Graham I knew how that charmer must have felt. If I had been in a position to compare notes with him, we would have agreed that the less we saw of adders in the future the better it would be for us.

Nobody could have charmed more wisely than me as I urged Herbert Graham to lower his price, and nobody could have stopped his ears more firmly than did that human serpent. Talk about someone not meeting you half-way; he didn't go an inch in the direction of coming to a peaceful settlement. Thirty-five quid, I mean to say. Absolutely monstrous. But that's what happens when you're up against it and the other fellow holds all the cards.

Haggling is a thing that takes it out of you, and it was a limp Bertram Wooster who after Graham and cat had set forth on their journey sat skimming listlessly through the opening pages of *By Order Of The Czar*. And I had read enough to make me wish I had taken out *The Mystery Of A Hansom Cab* instead, when the telephone rang.

It was, as I had feared, Aunt Dahlia. Sooner or later, I had of course realized, exchanges with the aged relative were inevitable, but I could have faced them better if they could have been postponed for a while. In my enfeebled condition I was in no shape to cope with aunts. A man who has just become engaged to a girl whose whole personality gives him a sinking feeling and who has had to pay thirty-five quid to a bloodsucker and another twopence to a lending library for a dud book is seldom in mid-season form.

The old ancestor, on the other hand, little knowing that she was about to get a sock on the jaw which would shake her to her foundation garments, was all lightheartedness and joviality.

'Hullo, fathead,' she said. 'What news on the Rialto?'

'What, what, where?' I responded, not getting it.

'The cat. Has he brought it?'

'Yes.'

'Is it in your bosom?'

I saw the time had come. Shrink though I might from revealing the awful truth, it had to be done. I took a deep breath. It was some small comfort to feel that she was at the end of the telephone wire a mile and a half away. You can never be certain what aunts will do when at close quarters. Far less provocation in my earlier days had led this one to buffet me soundly on the side of the head.

'No,' I said, 'it's gone.'

'Gone? Gone where?'

'Billy Graham has taken it back.'

'Taken it *back*?'

'To Eggesford Court. I told him to.'

'You *told* him to?'

'Yes. You see —'

That concluded for a considerable space of time my share in the duologue, for she got into high with the promptness which I had anticipated. She spoke as follows:

'Hell's bells! Ye gods! Angels and ministers of grace defend us! He brought the cat, and you deliberately turned it from your door, though you knew what it meant to me. Letting the side down! Failing me in my hour of need! Bringing my grey hairs in sorrow to the grave! And after all I've done for you, you miserable ungrateful worm. Do you remember me telling you that when you were a babe and suckling and looking, I may add in passing, like a badly poached egg, you nearly swallowed your rubber comforter, and if I hadn't jerked it out in time, you would have choked to death? It would go hard for you if you swallowed your rubber comforter now. I wouldn't stir a finger. Do you remember when you had measles and I gave up hours of my valuable time to playing tiddlywinks with you and letting you beat me without a murmur?'

I could have disputed that. My victories had been due entirely to skill. I haven't played much tiddlywinks lately, but in those boyhood days I was pretty hot stuff at the pastime. I did not mention this, however, because she was proceeding and I didn't like to interrupt the flow.

'Do you remember when you were at that private school of yours I used to send you parcels of food at enormous expense because you said you were about to expire from starvation? Do you remember when you were at Oxford —'

'Stop, aged r.,' I cried, for she had touched me deeply with these reminiscences of the young Wooster. 'You're breaking my heart.'

'You haven't got a heart. If you had, you wouldn't have driven that poor defenceless cat out into the snow. All I asked of you was to give it a bed in the spare room for a few days and so place my financial affairs on a sound basis, but you wouldn't do a trifling service for me which would have cost you nothing except a bob or two for milk and fish. What, I ask myself, has become of the old-fashioned nephew to whom his aunt's wishes were law? They don't seem to be making them nowadays.'

At this point Nature took its toll. She had to pause to take in breath, and I was enabled to speak.

'Old blood relation,' I said, 'you are under a what-is-it.'

'What is what?'

'The thing people get under. It's on the tip of my tongue. Begins with mis. Ah, I've got it, misapprehension. I've heard Jeeves use the word. Your view of my behaviour with the above cat is all cockeyed. I disapproved of your pinching it, because I felt that such an action stained the escutcheon of the Woosters, but I would have given it bed and board, however reluctantly, had it not been for Plank.'

'Plank?'

'Major Plank the explorer.'

'What's he got to do with it?'

'Everything. You've probably heard of Major Plank.'

'I haven't.'

'Well, he's one of those chaps who have native bearers and things and go exploring. Who was it out in Africa somewhere who met the other fellow and presumed he was Doctor something? Plank is, or was, in the same line of business.'

A snort came over the wire, nearly fusing it.

'Bertie,' said the blood relation, now having taken aboard an adequate supply of air, 'I am hampered by being at the other end of the telephone, but were I within reach of you I would give you one on the side of the head which you wouldn't forget in a hurry. Tell me in a few simple words what you think you're talking about.'

'I'm talking about Plank. And what I'm trying to establish is that Plank, though an explorer, is not exploring now. He is staying with Cook at Eggesford Court.'

'So what?'

'So jolly well this. He dropped in on me shortly after Billy Graham had clocked in and left the cat. It was with Jeeves in the kitchen, having one for the tonsils. And while Plank was there it yowled, and Plank of course heard it. You don't need to be told the upshot. Plank goes back to Cook, tells him he thought he heard a cat at Wooster's address, and Cook, already suspicious of me after our unfortunate encounter, comes down here like a wolf on the fold, his cohorts all gleaming with purple and gold. I ought to add that I told Plank that the cat he heard was not a cat but Jeeves imitating cats, and he believed it all right because explorers are simple-minded bozos who believe everything they're told, but will the story get over with Cook? Not a hope. There was nothing for me to do but tell Billy Graham to return the cat.'

I suppose one of the top-notch barristers could have put it more clearly, but not much more. She was silent for a space. Musing, no doubt, and weighing this against that. Finally she spoke.

'I see.'

'Good.'

'You appear not to have been such a non-co-operative hellhound as I thought you were.'

'Excellent.'

'Sorry I ticked you off with such vigour.'

'Quite all right, aged relative. *Tout comprendre c'est tout pardonner.*'

'Yes, I suppose it was the only thing you could do. But don't expect any hallelujahs from me. My whole plan of campaign has gone phut.'

'Oh, I don't know. Perhaps everything will be all right. Simla may win anyway.'

'Yes, but one did like to feel that one was betting on a certainty. It's no good trying to cheer me up. I feel awful.'

'Me, too.'

'What's wrong with you?'

'I'm engaged to be married to a girl I can't stand the sight of.'

'What, another? Who is it this time?'

'Vanessa Cook.'

'Any relation to old Cook?'

'His daughter.'

'How did it happen?'

'I proposed to her a year ago, and she turned me down, and just now she blew in and said she had changed her mind and would marry me. Came as a nasty shock.'

'You should have told her to go and boil her head.'

'I couldn't.'

'Why couldn't you?'

'Not *preux.*'

'Not what?'

'*Preux.* P for potted meat, r for rissole, e for egg nog, and so on. You've heard of a *preux chevalier*? It is my aim to be one.'

'Oh, well, if you go about being *Preux,* you must expect to get into trouble. But I wouldn't worry. You're bound to wriggle out of it somehow. You told me once that you had faith in your star. The girls you've been engaged to and have escaped from would reach, if placed end to end, from Piccadilly to Hyde Park Corner. I won't believe you're married till I see the bishop and assistant clergy mopping their foreheads and saying, "Well, that's that. We've really got the young blighter off at last."'

And with these words of cheer she rang off.

You would rather have expected that it would have been with a light heart that I returned to *By Order Of The Czar.* Such, however, was not the case. I had squared myself with the old flesh-and-blood and so had put a stopper on her wrath, a continuance of which might have resulted in her barring me from her table for an indefinite period, thus depriving me of the masterpieces of her French chef Anatole, God's gift to the gastric juices, but, as I say, the h. was not l. I could not but mourn for the collapse of the aged relative's hopes and dreams, a collapse for which I, though a mere toy in the hands of Fate, was bound to consider myself responsible.

I said as much to Jeeves when he came in with the materials for the pre-dinner cocktail.

'My heart is heavy, Jeeves,' I said, after expressing gratification at the sight of the fixings.

'Indeed, sir? Why is that?'

'I have just been having a painful scene with Aunt Dahlia. Well, when I say scene that's not quite the right word, the conversation having been conducted over the telephone. Did Graham get off all right?'

'Yes, sir.'

'Accompanied by cat?'

'Yes, sir.'

'That's what I was telling her, and she became a bit emotional. You never hunted with the Quorn or the Pytchley, did you, Jeeves? It seems to do something to the vocabulary. Lends a speaker eloquence. The old flesh-and-blood didn't have to pause to pick her words, they came out like bullets from a machine-gun. I was thankful we weren't talking face to face. Goodness knows what might have happened if we had been.'

'You should have told Mrs Travers the facts relating to Major Plank, sir.'

'I did, the moment I could get a word in edgeways, and it was that that acted like . . . like what?'

'Balm in Gilead, sir?'

'Exactly. I was going to say manna in the wilderness, but balm in Gilead hits it off better. She calmed down and admitted that I couldn't have done anything else but return the cat.'

'Most satisfactory, sir.'

'Yes, that part of it is all pretty smooth, but there's one other thing that's weighing on me a bit. I'm engaged to be married.'

CHAPTER FOURTEEN

As always when I tell him I'm engaged to be married, he betrayed no emotion, continuing to look as if he had been stuffed by a good taxidermist. It is not his place, he would say if you asked him, to go beyond the basic formalities on these occasions.

'Indeed, sir?' he said.

Usually this about covers it, and I don't discuss my predicament with him. I feel it wouldn't be seemly, if that's the word, and I know he would feel it wouldn't be seemly, so with both of us feeling it wouldn't be seemly we talk of other matters.

But this was a special occasion. Never before had I become betrothed to someone who would make me cut out smoking and cocktails, and in my opinion this made the subject a legitimate one for debate. When you're up against it as I was, it is essential to exchange views with a mastermind, if you can get hold of one, however unseemly it may be.

So when he added, 'May I offer my congratulations, sir,' I replied with lines which were not on the routine.

'No, Jeeves, you may not, not by a jugful. You see before you a man who is as near to being what is known as a toad at

Harrow as a man can be who was educated at Eton. I'm in sore straits, Jeeves.'

'I am sorry to hear that, sir.'

'You'll be sorrier when I explain further. Have you ever seen a garrison besieged by howling savages, with their ammunition down to the last box of cartridges, the water supply giving out and the United States Marines nowhere in sight?'

'Not to my recollection, sir.'

'Well, my position is roughly that of such a garrison, except that compared with me they're sitting pretty. Compared with me they haven't a thing to worry about.'

'You fill me with alarm, sir.'

'I bet I do, and I haven't even started yet. I will begin by saying that Miss Cook, to whom I'm engaged, is a lady for whom I have the utmost esteem and respect, but on certain matters we do not . . . what's the expression?'

'See eye to eye, sir?'

'That's right. And unfortunately those matters are the what-d'you-call-it of my whole policy. What is it that policies have?'

'I think the word for which you are groping, sir, may possibly be cornerstone.'

'Thank you, Jeeves. She disapproves of a variety of things which are the cornerstone of my policy. Marriage with her must inevitably mean that I shall have to cast them from my life, for she has a will of iron and will have no difficulty in making her husband jump through hoops and snap sugar off his nose. You get what I mean?'

'I do, sir. A very colourful image.'

'Cocktails, for instance, will be barred. She says they are bad for the liver. Have you noticed, by the way, how frightfully lax everything's getting now? In Queen Victoria's day a girl would never have dreamed of mentioning livers in mixed company.'

'Very true, sir. *Tempora mutantur, nos et mutamur in illis.*'

'That, however, is not the worst.'

'You horrify me, sir.'

'At a pinch I could do without cocktails. It would be agony, but we Woosters can rough it. But she says I must give up smoking.'

'This was indeed the most unkindest cut of all, sir.'

'Give up smoking, Jeeves!'

'Yes, sir. You will notice that I am shuddering.'

'The trouble is that she is greatly under the influence of a pal of hers called Tolstoy. I've never met him, but he seems to have the most extraordinary ideas. You won't believe this, Jeeves, but he says that no one needs to smoke, as equal pleasure can be obtained by twirling the fingers. The man must be an ass. Imagine a posh public dinner – one of those "decorations will be worn" things. The royal toast has been drunk, strong men are licking their lips at the thought of cigars, and the toastmaster bellows "Gentlemen, you may twirl your fingers." Don't tell me there wouldn't be a flat feeling, a sense of disappointment. Do you know anything about this fellow Tolstoy? You ever heard of him?'

'Oh, yes, sir. He was a very famous Russian novelist.'

'Russian, eh? Well, there you are. And a novelist? He didn't write *By Order Of The Czar*, did he?'

'I believe not, sir.'

'I thought he might have under another name. You say "was". Is he no longer with us?'

'No, sir. He died some years ago.'

'Good for him. Twirl your fingers! Too absurd. I'd laugh

only she says I mustn't laugh because another pal of hers, called Chesterfield, didn't. Well, she needn't worry. The way things are shaping I haven't anything to laugh about. For I've not mentioned the principal objection to the marriage. Don't jump to the hasty conclusion that I mean because a father-in-law like Cook is included in the package deal. I grant you that that's enough by itself to darken the horizon, but what's on my mind is the thought of Orlo Porter.'

'Ah, yes, sir.'

I gave him an austere look.

'If you can't say anything better than "Ah, yes", Jeeves, say nothing.'

'Very good, sir.'

'The thought, as I was saying, of Orlo Porter. We have already touched on his testy disposition, the iron-bandlike muscles of his brawny arms, and his jealousy. The mere suspicion that I was inflicting my beastly society, as he put it, on Miss Cook was enough to make him tell me that he would tear out my insides with his bare hands. What'll he do when he finds I'm engaged to her?'

'Surely, sir, the lady having so unequivocally rejected him, he can scarcely blame you —'

'For filling the vacant spot? Don't you believe it. He'll take it for granted that I persuaded her to give him the pink slip. Nothing will drive it out of his nut. The belief that I'm a Grade A snake in the grass, and we all know what to expect from snakes in the g. No, we have got to be frightfully subtle and think of some plan for drawing his fangs. Otherwise my insides won't be worth a moment's purchase.'

I was about to go on to ask him if he still had the cosh — or blackjack, to use the American term — which he had taken away from Aunt Dahlia's son Bonzo some months previously. Bonzo had bought it to use on a schoolmate he disliked, and we all thought he would be better without it. It was, of course, precisely what I needed to ease the tenseness of the O. Porter situation. Armed with this weapon, I could defy O. Porter without a qualm. But before I could speak the telephone tootled in the hall. I waved a hand in its direction.

'Answer that, would you mind, Jeeves, and say I've gone for a brisk walk, as recommended by my medical adviser. It'll be Aunt Dahlia, and though she was in a reasonable frame of mind at the conclusion of our recent talk, there's no telling how long these reasonable frames of mind will last.'

'Very good, sir.'

'You know what women are.'

'I do, indeed, sir.'

'Especially aunts.'

'Yes, sir. My aunt –'

'Tell me all about her later.'

'Any time you wish, sir.'

I remember Jeeves once saying of my friend Catsmeat Potter-Pirbright – it was when a long shot he had backed had come in first by a head, only to be disqualified owing to some infringement of the rules by its jockey – that melancholy had marked him for her own, and it was the same with me now as I sat totting up the score and realizing how extraordinarily deeply I had been plunged in the soup.

Compared with other items on the list of my troubles it was perhaps a minor cause for melancholy that the old ancestor should be trying to get me on the telephone. Nevertheless, it added one more thing to worry about. It could only mean, I felt, that she had come out of the amiable mood she had been in when last heard from and had thought of a lot more nasty cracks to make on the subject of my failure to reach the standard which she considered adequate in a nephew. And I was in no shape to listen to destructive criticism when we next met, especially when delivered by a voice trained by years of shouting 'Gone away' at foxes to reduce the hearer's nervous system to pulp.

When, therefore, Jeeves returned, my first observation was:

'What did she say?'

'It was not Mrs Travers, sir, it was Mr Porter.'

I was more thankful than ever that I had got him to answer the phone.

'Well, what did *he* say?' I asked, though I could have made a rough guess.

'I regret that I am not able to report the entire conversation verbatim, sir. I found the gentleman incoherent at the outset. I gathered that he was under the impression that he was addressing you, and emotion interfered with the clarity of his diction. I informed him of my identity, and he moderated his verbal speed. I was thus enabled to follow him. He gave me several messages to give to you.'

'Messages?'

'Yes, sir, embodying what he proposed to do to you when next you met. His remarks were in the main of a crudely surgical nature, and many of the plans he outlined would be extremely difficult to put into practice. His threat, for instance, to pull off your head and make you swallow it.'

'He said that?'

'Among other things more or less on the same trend. But you need have no apprehension, sir.'

It shows the state to which the slings and arrows of

outrageous fortune, as somebody called them, had reduced me that I didn't laugh a hacking laugh at this. I didn't even utter a sardonic 'Oh, yeah' or 'Says you'. I merely buried the face in the hands, and he continued:

'Before I left the room you were speaking of the necessity of drawing Mr Porter's fangs, as you very aptly put it. It gives me great pleasure to say that I have succeeded in doing this.'

I thought I couldn't have heard him correctly, and asked him to repeat his amazing statement. He did so, and I looked at him astounded. You might suppose that I would have been used by this time to seeing him pull rabbits out of a hat with a flick of the wrist and solve in a flash problems which had defied the best efforts of the finest minds, but it always comes fresh to me, depriving me of breath and causing the eyeballs to rotate in the parent sockets.

Then I saw what must be behind the easy confidence with which he had spoken.

'So you remembered the cosh?' I said.

'Sir?'

'And you have it in your possession.'

'I do not quite understand you, sir.'

'I thought you meant that you still had that cosh which you took away from Aunt Dahlia's Bonzo and were going to give it to me so that I would be armed when Porter made his spring.'

'Oh, no, sir. The instrument to which you refer is among my effects at our London residence.'

'Then how did you draw his fangs?'

'By reminding him that you have taken out an accident policy with him and drawing his attention to the inevitable displeasure of his employers if through him they were mulcted in a substantial sum of money. I had little difficulty in persuading the gentleman that anything in the nature of aggressive action on his part would be a mistake.'

I repeated the stare. His resource and ingenuity had stunned me.

'Jeeves,' I said, 'your resource and ingenuity have stunned me. Porter is baffled.'

'Yes, sir.'

'Unless you would prefer "thwarted".'

'Baffled I think is stronger.'

'Talk of drawing his fangs. His dentist will have to fit him with a completely new set.'

'Yes, sir, but we must not forget that the removal of Mr Porter as a menace is only half a battle. I hesitate to touch on a delicate subject . . .'

'Touch on, Jeeves.'

'But I gathered, partly from what you were saying and partly from the tone of your voice as you said it when you were speaking of her plans for your future, that the idea of marriage with Miss Cook is not wholly agreeable to you, and it occurred to me that much unpleasantness would be avoided, were the lady and Mr Porter to be reconciled.'

'It would indeed. But –'

'You were about to say, sir, that in your opinion the rift is too serious for that?'

'Well, isn't it?'

'I think not.'

'Your blow by blow description of the hostilities certainly gave me the impression that they had parted brass rags pretty finally. How about that lily-livered poltroon?'

'You have placed your finger on the real trouble, sir. Miss

Cook applied that term to Mr Porter because of his refusal to approach her father and demand the money which the latter is holding in trust for him.'

'Well, according to you he said he wouldn't approach her father in a million years.'

'The situation has been changed by your becoming affianced to the woman he loves. To restore himself to Miss Cook's esteem he would face perils from which formerly he shrank.'

I got what he meant, but I didn't buy the idea. I still saw Orlo shrinking.

'Furthermore, sir, if you were to go to Mr Porter and point out to him that success might crown his efforts if he were to choose a moment shortly after dinner to approach Mr Cook, he would take the risk. A gentleman mellowed by a good dinner is always more amenable to overtures of any kind than one who is waiting for his food, as I understood from his conversation that Mr Cook was when Mr Porter discussed business with him on a former occasion.'

I started visibly. He had electrified me.

'Jeeves,' I said, 'I believe you've got something.'

'I think so, sir.'

'I'll go and see Porter at once. He's probably at the Goose and Grasshopper drowning his sorrows in gin and ginger ale. And let me say once more that you stand alone. You have made my day. I wish there was something I could do for you by way of return.'

'There is, sir.'

'It's yours, even unto half my kingdom. Give me a name.'

'I should be extremely grateful if you would allow me to spend the night at my aunt's.'

'You want to go to Liverpool? A long journey.'

'No, sir. My aunt returned this morning and is at her home in the village.'

'Then go to her, Jeeves, and heaven smile upon your reunion.'

'Thank you very much, sir. Should you have need of my services, the address is Balmoral, Mafeking Road, care of Mrs P. B. Pigott.'

'Oh, she isn't a Jeeves?'

'No, sir.'

He shimmered out, to return a moment later with the information that Mr Graham was in the kitchen and would be glad of a word with me. And it shows the extent to which the strain and rush of life at Maiden Eggesford had taken its toll that for a moment the name conveyed nothing to me. Then memory returned to its throne, and I felt as anxious to see Mr Graham as he apparently was to see me. Such was my confidence in him as a returner of cats that I could not imagine him failing in his mission, but I was naturally anxious to have the full details.

'In the kitchen, you say?'

'Yes, sir.'

'Then bung him in, Jeeves. There is no one I'd rather give audience to.'

And the hour, which was getting on for six o'clock, produced the man.

I was struck, as before, by the intense respectability of his appearance. He looked as though no rabbit or pheasant need entertain the slightest tremors in his presence, and one could readily picture him as the backbone of the choir when anthem time came along. His gentle 'Good evening, sir' was a treat to listen to.

'Good evening,' I said in my turn. 'Well? You accomplished your mission? The cat is back at the old stand?'

His eyes darkened, as if I had brought to the surface a secret sorrow.

'Well, yes and no, sir.'

'How do you mean, yes and no?'

'To the first of your questions the answer is in the affirmative. I did accomplish my mission. But unfortunately the cat is not at the old stand.'

'I don't get you.'

'It is here, sir, in your kitchen. I took it to Eggesford Court as per contract and released it near the stables and started on my homeward journey, happy to have earned the money which you so generously paid me for my services. Picture my astonishment and dismay when on reaching the village I discovered that the cat had followed me. It is a very affectionate animal, and we had become great friends. Would you wish me to take it back again? Of course I should not feel justified in charging my full fee, so shall we say ten pounds?'

If you want to know how this proposition affected me, I can put it in a nutshell by saying that I read him like a book. Many people are led by my frank and open countenance into thinking that I am one of the mugs, but I know a twister when I see one and I was in no doubt that one of these stood before me now.

What stopped me drawing myself to my full height and denouncing him was the reflection that the blighter had me in a cleft stick. Refusal to come across would mean him going to Pop Cook and getting a handsome fee from him for revealing that the aged relative had paid him to purloin the cat, and in spite of what she had said about her popularity in Maiden

Eggesford, resulting from her rendering 'Every Nice Girl Loves A Sailor' in a sailor suit, I knew that her name would be mud. I still wasn't sure she couldn't even be jugged, and what a sock in the eye that would give Uncle Tom's digestion.

I disbursed the tenner. Not blithely, but I disbursed it, and he went on his way.

For some little time after he had left I sat wrapped in thought. And then, just as I was getting up to go and see Orlo, in came Vanessa Cook.

CHAPTER FIFTEEN

She was accompanied by a dog of about the size of a young elephant, yellow in colour and with large ears sticking up, with whom I would willingly have fraternized, but after drinking in the delicious scent of my trouser legs for a brief moment it saw something out in the street which aroused its interest and left us.

Vanessa, meanwhile, had picked up my *By Order Of The Czar*, and I could see by the way she sniffed that she was about to become critical. There had always been a strong strain of book-reviewer blood in her.

'Trash,' she said. 'It really is time you began reading something worth while. I don't expect you to start off with Turgenev and Dostoievsky' she said, evidently alluding to a couple of Russian exiles she had met in London who did a bit of writing on the side, 'but there are plenty of good books which are easier and at the same time educational. I have brought one with me,' she went on, and I saw that she was holding a slim volume bound in limp purple leather with some sort of decoration in gold on the cover, and I shuddered strongly. To a man who has seen as much of life as I have there is always something sinister in a book bound in limp purple leather. 'It is a collection of whimsical essays, *The Prose Ramblings Of A Rhymester*, by Reginald Sprockett, a brilliant young poet from whom the critics expect great things. His style has been much praised, but it is the thought in these little gems to which I particularly call your attention. I will leave them here. I must be off. I only came to bring you the book . . .'

You probably think I reeled beneath this blow, but actually my heart was not so heavy as it might have been, for my quick brain had perceived how this would do me a bit of good. The revolting object would make an admirable Christmas present for my Aunt Agatha, always a difficult person to find Yule-Tide gifts for. I was warming myself with this thought, when Vanessa continued.

'Be very careful not to lose it. It has Reginald's autograph in it,' and glancing at the title page I saw that this was indeed so, which would have bucked Aunt Agatha up no little, but in addition to inscribing the slim volume with his own foul name the blighter had inscribed Vanessa's. 'To Vanessa, the fairest of the fair, from a devoted admirer,' he had written, dishing my plans completely. That was when my heart got heavy again. For though she hadn't definitely said so, something told me that later on I would be expected to pass an examination on the little opus, and failure would have the worst effects.

Having said she must be off, she naturally stayed on for another half-hour, much of which time was devoted to pointing out additional defects in my spiritual make-up which had occurred to her since our last meeting. It just showed how strong the missionary spirit can be in women that she could contemplate the idea of teaming up with a dubious character like B. Wooster. Her best friends would have warned her against it. 'Cast him into outer darkness where there is weeping and gnashing of teeth,' they would have said. 'No good trying to patch him up, he's hopeless.'

It was my membership of the Drones Club that now formed the basis of her observations. She didn't like the Drones Club, and she made it quite clear that at the conclusion of the honeymoon I would cross its threshold only over her dead body.

So, reckoning up the final score, the Bertram Wooster who signed the charge sheet in the vestry after the wedding ceremony would be a non-smoker, a teetotaller (for I knew it would come to that) and an ex-member of the Drones, in other words a mere shell of his former self. Little wonder that, as I listened to her, I gulped as Plank's native bearer must have done when they were getting ready to bury him before sundown.

The prospect appalled me, and while it was appalling me Vanessa moved to the door, this time apparently really intending to be off. And she had opened the door, Bertram much too much of a shell of his former self to open it for her, when she started back with a gasping cry.

'Father!' she cried gaspingly. 'He's coming up the garden path.'

'He's coming up the garden *path*?' I said. I was at a loss to imagine why Pop Cook should be calling on me. I mean to say we weren't on those terms.

'He's stopped to tie his boot lace,' she cried, gaspingly as before, and that concluded her share of the dialogue. With no further words she bounded into the kitchen like a fox pursued by both the Quorn and the Pytchley, slamming the door behind her.

I could appreciate her emotion. She was aware of her parent's distaste for the last of the Woosters, a distaste so marked that he turned mauve and swallowed his lunch the wrong way at the mention of my name, and *chez* me was the last place he would wish to find her. Orlo Porter had thought the worst on learning of what he called her clandestine visits to the Wooster home, and a father would, of course, think worse than Orlo. Pure though I was as the driven s., a fat chance I had of persuading him that I wasn't a modern Casa something. Not Casabianca. That was the chap who stood on the burning deck. Casanova. I knew I'd get it.

And what he would do to Vanessa in his wrath would be plenty. She was, as I have made clear, a proud beauty, but a father of the calibre of Pop Cook can make even a proud beauty wish she had thought twice before blotting her copybook. He may not be able any longer to whale the tar out of her with his walking stick as in the good old days, but he can cut off her pocket money and send her to stay with her grandmother at Tunbridge Wells, where she will have to look after seven cats and attend divine service three times on Sunday. Yes, one could understand her being perturbed on seeing him tying up his boot lace outside Wee Nooke, which, I forgot to mention earlier, was the name of my GHQ. (It had been built, I learned subsequently, for a female cousin of Mrs Briscoe's who painted water colours.)

And if she was perturbed, I was on the perturbed side, too. It was with some trepidation – in fact, quite a lot of it – that I awaited my visitor's arrival, a trepidation that was not diminished when I saw that he had brought his hunting crop with him.

I hadn't taken to him much at our previous meeting, and I had the feeling that I wasn't going to get very fond of him now, but I will say this for him, that he didn't waste time. He was a man of quick, decisive speech who had no use for tedious preliminaries but came to the point at once. I suppose you have to in order to run a big business successfully.

'Well, Mr Wooster, as I understand you are calling yourself now, it may interest you to know that Major Plank, who had lost his memory, recovered it last night, and he told me all about you.'

It was a nasty knock, and the fact that I had been expecting it didn't make it any better. Oddly enough, I felt no animosity towards Cook, holding Plank the bloke responsible for this awkward situation. Roaming through Africa knee-deep in poisonous snakes of every description and with more man-eating pumas around than you could shake a stick at, he could so easily have passed away, regretted by all. Instead of which, he survived and went about making life tough for harmless typical young men about town who simply wanted to be left alone to restore their delicate health.

Cook was continuing, and getting nastier every moment.

'You are a notorious crook, known to your associates as Alpine Joe, and your latest crime was to try to sell Major Plank a valuable statuette which you had stolen from Sir Watkyn Bassett of Totleigh Towers. You were arrested by Inspector Witherspoon of Scotland Yard, fortunately before you had accomplished your nefarious ends. I presume from the fact that you are at large that you have served your sentence, and you are now in the pay of Colonel Briscoe, who has employed you to steal my cat. Have you anything to say?'

'Yes,' I said.

'No, you haven't,' he said.

'I can explain everything,' I said.

'No, you can't,' he said.

And, by Jove, I suddenly realized I couldn't. It would have involved a long character analysis of Sir Watkyn Bassett, another of my Uncle Tom, a third of Stephanie (Stiffy) Byng, now Mrs Stinker Pinker, a fourth of Jeeves, and would have taken about two hours and a quarter, provided he listened attentively and didn't interrupt, which of course he would have done.

Matters, therefore, seemed to be at what you might call a deadlock, and the thought had suggested itself to me that my best plan would be to leave his presence and start running and keep on running till I reached the northern fringe of Scotland, when a noise like an explosion in a gas works broke in on my reverie, and I saw that he was holding the slim volume which Vanessa, the silly ass, had omitted to take off-stage with her.

'This book!' he yowled.

I did my best.

'Ah, yes,' I said, 'Reggie Sprockett's latest. I always keep up with his work. A brilliant young poet of whom the critics expect great things. These, in case you are interested, are whimsical essays. They are superb. Not only the style, but the thought in these little gems . . .'

My voice died away. I had been about to urge him to buy a copy, but I saw that he was not in the mood. He was staring at the opening page with its inscription, and I knew that words would be wasted, as the expression is.

He gave the hunting crop a twitch.

'My daughter has been here.'

'She did look in.'

'Ha!'

I knew what that 'Ha!' meant. It was short for 'I shall now thrash you within an inch of your life.' A moment later he used the longer version, as if in doubt as to whether he had made himself clear.

If you were to come to me and say 'Wooster, to settle a bet, which would you estimate is to be preferred, having your insides torn out by somebody's bare hands or being thrashed within an inch of your life?', I would find it difficult to decide. Both are things you'd rather have happen to another chap. But I think I would give my vote in favour of the last-named, always provided the other fellow was doing it in a small room, for there he would find that he had set himself a testing task. The dimensions of the sitting-room of Wee Nooke did not permit of a full swing. Cook had to confine himself to chip shots, which an agile person like myself had little difficulty in eluding.

I eluded them, therefore, with no great expenditure of physical effort, but I would be deceiving my public if I said that I was enjoying the episode. It offends one's pride when one has to leap like a lamb in Springtime at the bidding of an elderly little Gawd-help-us with whom it is impossible to reason. And it was plain that Cook in his present frame of mind wouldn't recognize reason if you served it up to him in an individual plate with watercress round it.

That, of course, was what prevented me fulfilling myself in the encounter, the fact that he *was* an elderly little Gawd-help-us. It was the combination of age and size that kept me from giving of my best. I might – indeed I would – have dotted in the eye a small young Gawd-help-us or a Gawd-help-us of riper years of the large economy size, but I couldn't possibly get tough with an undersized little squirt who would never see fifty-five again. The chivalry of the Woosters couldn't ever contemplate such an action.

I thought once or twice of adopting the policy which had occurred to me at the outset – viz. running up to the north of Scotland. I had often wondered, when I read about fellows getting horsewhipped on the steps of their club, why they didn't just go up the steps and into the club, knowing that the chap behind the horsewhip wasn't a member and wouldn't have a chance of getting past the hall porter.

But the catch was that running up to Scotland would mean turning my back, a fatal move. So we just carried on with our rhythmic dance till my guardian angel, who until now had just been sitting there, decided – and about time, too – to take a hand in the proceedings. As might have been expected in a cottage called Wee Nooke, there was a grandfather clock over against the wall, and he now arranged that Cook should bump into this and come a purler. And while he was still on the floor I acted with the true Wooster resource.

I have stated that the previous owner of Wee Nooke expressed herself as a rule in water colours, but on one occasion she had changed her act. Over the mantelpiece there hung a large oil painting depicting a bloke in a three-cornered hat and riding breeches in conference with a girl in a bonnet and what looked like muslin, and as it caught my eye I suddenly remembered Gussie Fink-Nottle and the portrait at Aunt Dahlia's place in Worcestershire.

Gussie – stop me if you've heard this before – while closely pursued by Spode, now Lord Sidcup, who, if memory serves me aright, wanted to break his neck, had taken refuge in my bedroom and was on the point of having his neck broken when he plucked a picture from the wall and brought it down on Spode's head. The head came through the canvas, and Spode, momentarily bewildered at finding himself wearing a portrait of one of Uncle Tom's ancestors round his neck like an Elizabethan ruff, gave me the opportunity of snatching a sheet from the bed and enveloping him in it, rendering him null and void, as the expression is.

I went through a precisely similar routine now, first applying the picture and then the tablecloth. After which I withdrew and went off to the Goose and Grasshopper to see Orlo.

CHAPTER SIXTEEN

Anybody not in possession of the facts would probably have been appalled at my rashness in placing myself within disembowelling range of Orlo Porter, feeling that I was tempting fate, and in about two ticks would be wishing I hadn't.

But I, strong in the knowledge that Orlo P. had been reduced to the level of a fifth-rate power, was able to approach the coming interview in a bumps-a-daisy spirit which might quite easily have led to my bursting into song.

Orlo, as I had predicted, was in the bar having a gin and ginger. He lowered the beaker as I drew near and regarded me in a squiggle-eyed manner like a fastidious luncher observing a caterpillar in his salad.

'Oh, it's you,' he said.

I conceded this, for he was right. No argument about it. Assured that he wasn't looking squiggle-eyed at the wrong chap, he proceeded.

'What do you want?'

'A word with you.'

'So you have come to gloat?'

'Certainly not, Porter,' I said, 'when you hear what I have to say, you will start skipping like the high hills, not that I've ever seen high hills skip, or low hills for that matter. Porter, what would you say if I told you all your troubles, all the little odds and ends that are bothering you now, would be over 'ere yonder sun had set?'

'It has set.'

'Oh, has it? I didn't notice.'

'And it is getting on for dinner time. So if you will kindly get the hell out of here –'

'Not till I have spoken.'

'Are you going to speak some *more*?'

'Lots more. Let us examine the position you and I are in calmly, and in a judicial spirit. Vanessa Cook has told me she will marry me, and you are probably looking on me as a snake in the grass. Well, let me tell you that any resemblance between me and a snake in the grass is purely coincidental. I couldn't issue a *nolle prosequi*, could I, when she said that? Of course not. But all the while I was right-hoing I felt I was behaving like a louse.'

'You are a louse.'

'No, that's where you make your error, Porter. I am a man of sensibility, and a man of sensibility does not marry a girl who's in love with somebody else. He gives her up.'

He finished his gin and ginger, and choked on it as he suddenly got the gist.

'You would give her up to me?'

'Absolutely.'

'But, Wooster, this is noble. I'm sorry I said you were a louse.'

'Quite all right. Sort of mistake anyone might make.'

'You remind me of Cyrano de Bergerac.'

'One has one's code.'

He had been all smiles – or pretty nearly all smiles – up to this point, but now melancholy marked him for her own again. He heaved a sigh, as if he had found a dead mouse at the bottom of his tankard.

'It would be useless for you to make this sacrifice, Wooster. Vanessa would never marry me.'

'Of course she would.'

'You weren't there when she broke the engagement.'

'My representative was. At least he was listening at the door.'

'Then you know the general run of the thing.'

'He gave me a full report.'

'And you say she still loves me?'

'Like a ton of bricks. Love cannot be extinguished by a potty little lovers' quarrel.'

'Potty little lovers' quarrel my left eyeball. She called me a lily-livered poltroon. And a sleekit timorous cowering beastie. One wonders where she picks up such expressions. And all because I refused to go to old Cook and demand my money. I'd been to him once and asked him in the most civil manner to cough up, and she wanted me to go again and this time to thump the table and generally throw my weight about.'

'You should, Orlo. That's just what you ought to do. What happened last time?'

'He flatly refused.'

'How flatly?'

'Very flatly. And it would be the same if I went again.'

He had given me the cue I wanted. I had been wondering how best to introduce what I had in mind. I smiled one of my subtle smiles, and he asked me what I was grinning about.

'Not if you select your time properly,' I said. 'What time was it you made your other try?'

'About five in the afternoon.'

'As I suspected. No wonder he gave you the bum's rush. Five in the afternoon is when a man's sunny disposition is down in the lowest brackets. Lunch wore off hours ago, and cocktails are not yet in sight. He isn't in the mood to oblige anyone about anything. Cook may be a hard-boiled egg, but dinner softens the hardest. Approach him when he is full to the brim, and you'll be surprised. Fellows at the Drones have told me that, applying after he had tucked into the evening meal, they have got substantial loans out of Oofy Prosser.'

'Who is Oofy Prosser?'

'The club millionaire, a man who by daylight watches his disbursement like a hawk. Cook is probably just the same. Tails up, Porter. Get cracking. Be bloody, bold and resolute,' I said, remembering a gag from that play *Macbeth*, which I was mentioning some while back.

He was impressed, as who would not have been. His face lit up as if someone had pressed a button.

'Wooster,' he said, 'you're right. You have shown me the way. You have made my path straight. Thank you, Wooster, old man.'

'Not at all, Porter, old chap.'

'It's an extraordinary thing; anyone looking at you would write you off as a brainless nincompoop with about as much intelligence as a dead rabbit.'

'Thank you, Porter, old chap.'

'Not at all, Wooster, old man. Whereas all the time you have this amazing insight into human psychology.'

'I have hidden depths, would you say?'

'You bet you have, Wooster, old horse.'

And in another jiffy he was pressing a gin and ginger on me as if we had been bosom pals for years and the subject of my insides had never come up between us.

Returning to Wee Nooke some twenty minutes later after what had practically amounted to a love-feast, I had that jolly feeling you don't often get nowadays that God was in his Heaven and all right with the world, as the fellow said. I counted my blessings one by one and found the sum total most satisfactory. All was quiet on the Porter front, Billy Graham was even now returning the cat to its little circle at Eggesford Court, Porter and Vanessa Cook would soon be sweethearts again, and if my popularity with Pop Cook was at a low ebb, rendering unlikely any chance of a present from him next Christmas, that was a small flaw in the ointment. Or is it fly? I never can remember. Everything, in short, was just like Mother makes it, and it was a blithe B. Wooster who, hearing the telephone tootle, went to answer it with, as you might say, a song on his lips.

It was the aged relative, and the dullest ear could have spotted that she was in something of a doodah. For some moments after we had established connection she confined herself to gasps and gurgles such as might have proceeded from some strong swimmer in his agony.

'Hullo,' I said. 'Is something up?'

In the course of this narrative I have had occasion to mention several hacking laughs, but for sheer rasp and explosiveness the one the old ancestor emitted at these words topped the lot.

'Something up?' she boomed. 'You would say a thing like

that when I'm nearly off my rocker. Has that cat been returned to store yet?'

'Billy Graham is in full control.'

'You mean he hasn't started yet?'

'Yes, and come back. But unfortunately the cat followed him. So he says. Anyway, he arrived here with it in close attendance, and he has now taken it off again. He's probably decanting the animal at this moment. But why the agitation?'

'I'll tell you why the agitation. If that cat is not back where it belongs immediately, if not sooner, ruin stares me in the eyeball and Tom is in for the worst attack of indigestion he has had since the time he ate all that lobster at his club. And only myself to blame.'

'Did you say you were to blame?'

'Yes. Why?'

'I only wondered if I had heard you correctly.'

I have become so accustomed to being blamed for everything that goes wrong that her words had touched me deeply. You don't often find an aunt taking the rap when she has a nephew at her disposal to shove the thing on to. It is pretty universally agreed that that is what nephews are for. My voice shook a bit as I applied for further details.

'What seems to be the trouble?' I asked.

Aunts as a class are seldom good listeners. She did not answer the question, but embarked on what sounded as if it was going to be a lecture on conditions in her native land.

'I'll tell you what's wrong with the England of today, Bertie. There are too many people around with scruples and high principles and all that sort of guff. You can't do the simplest thing without somebody jumping on the back of your neck because you've offended against his blasted code of ethics.

You'd think a man like Jimmy Briscoe would be broadminded, but no. He couldn't have been more puff-faced if he'd been the Archbishop of Canterbury. You probably put the blame on his brother the vicar, but I don't agree. I can excuse him because it's his job to be finicky about things. But Jimmy! He made me feel as if I'd shot a fox or something. And it wasn't as if I was getting anything out of it. It was a pure act of kindness because I could see he had the interests of the organ at heart and was really worried about it. Dammit, St Francis of Assisi would have done the same and everybody would have said what a splendid chap he was and what a pity there weren't more like him, whereas the way Jimmy went on . . .'

I could see that if not checked with a firm hand this would continue for a goodish time.

'I'm sorry if I seem slow in the uptake, aged r.,' I said, 'but, if so, put it down to the fact that you appear to me to be delirious. Your words are like the crackling of thorns under the pot, as the fellow said. What on earth do you think you're talking about?'

'Haven't you been listening?'

'I have been listening, yes, but without coming within a mile and a quarter of getting the gist.'

'Oh, heavens, I might have known I would have to tell you in words of one syllable. Here's what's happened in simple language which even you can understand. I happened to be talking to the vicar, and he told me what a weight on his mind the church organ was, it being at its last gasp and no money to pay the vet., because he'd already touched Jimmy for quite a bit to mend the church roof, and if he tried to bite his ear again so soon after that, there would, he said, be hell to pay. So what the devil to do, he said, he didn't know.

'Well, you know me, Bertie. Being a woman with a heart like butter and always anxious to spread a little happiness as I pass by, I told him that if he wanted a bit of easy money, to put his shirt on Jimmy's Simla for the big race. And I told him about the cat, just to make it quite clear to him that he would be betting on a sure thing.'

'But –'

'Put a sock in it and listen. Can't you stop talking for half a second? I know what you were going to say – that you were returning the cat. But this was before you told me. So I went ahead, fearing nothing, just thinking of the happiness I was bringing into his life. I ought to have known that a clergyman was bound to have scruples, but it didn't occur to me at the time and to cut a long story short he went to Jimmy and spilled the beans, and Jimmy blew his top. "Take that cat back where it belongs," he said, and a lot of stuff about being shocked and horrified. Which wouldn't have mattered if he had confined himself to telling me what he thought of me, but he didn't. He said that if that cat wasn't back at Cook's within the hour he would scratch Simla's nomination. Yessir, he said Simla would not be among those present at the starting post, which meant that bang would go the vast sum I had put on his nose.'

'But –'

'Yes, I know you had told me you were sending the cat back, but how was I to be sure that, on thinking it over and realizing what a good thing you would be passing up, you hadn't changed your mind?'

I could see what she meant. A nephew with a lust for gold and lacking the Wooster play-the-game spirit might quite well have done as she said. No wonder she had been all of a doodah. It was a pleasure to set her mind at rest.

'It's quite all right, old ancestor,' I said. 'Billy Graham is already en route for the Cookeries, and ought to have got there by now.'

'Complete with cat?'

'To the last drop.'

'Not to worry?'

'Not as far as Simla getting scratched is concerned.'

'Well, that's a weight off my mind, though it's disappointing to feel that my bit of stuff isn't on a cert.'

'Teach you not to nobble horses.'

'Yes, there's that, I suppose.'

Some further talk followed, for an aunt who has got hold of a telephone receiver does not lightly relinquish it, but eventually she rang off, and I picked up *Daffodil Days* and gave it a casual glance.

Its contents proved even less fit for human consumption than I had expected. I turned away with rising nausea, and was thus enabled to get a good view of Herbert Graham, who was coming in from the kitchen.

The suddenness of his appearance, coupled with the fact that I had supposed him to be up at Eggesford Court, had made me bite my tongue, but in my concern I ignored the anguish.

'Good Lord!' I ejaculated, if that's the word.

'Sir?'

'Haven't you gone yet? You should have been there and back by this time.'

'Very true, sir, but something occurred which prevented me making the immediate start which I had intended.'

'What was that? Did they keep you a long time at the bank, counting your money?'

Bitter, yes, but I thought justified. Wasted, however, for he did not wince beneath my sarcasm.

'No, sir,' he replied. 'I bank in Bridmouth-on-Sea, and it is long past office hours. The occurrence to which I refer took place on these premises, in fact in this very room. I had gone to the kitchen to get the cat, which I had left there in its little basket, and I heard sounds proceeding from in here and assuming that you were not at home I went in to investigate, fearing that a burglar might have effected an entry, and there on the floor was a human form enveloped in a tablecloth. I raised this, and there underneath it was Mr Cook with a picture round his neck, vociferating something chronic.'

He paused, and I decided not to put him abreast. Never does to take fellows like Graham too fully into one's confidence.

'Wrapped in a tablecloth, was he?' I said nonchalantly. 'I suppose chaps like Cook are bound to get wrapped in tablecloths sooner or later.'

'The sight affected me profoundly.'

'I bet it did. Sights like that do give one a start. But you soon got over it, eh?'

'No, sir, I did not, and I'll tell you why I was what you might call stupefied. It was his language that did it chiefly. As I was saying, he expressed himself in a very violent manner, and I saw that it would be madness to proceed to Eggesford Court and possibly encounter him in this dangerous mood. I am a married man and have others to think of. So if you want that cat re-established in its former quarters, you'll have to get another operative to do it for you or else nip up to the Court and do it yourself.'

And while I looked at him with a wild surmise, silent upon

a sitting-room carpet in Maiden Eggesford, Somerset, he withdrew.

I was still gazing at the spot where he had been and thinking how crazy I must have been to let Jeeves wander off, frittering away his time whooping it up with aunts, when I might have known I was bound to need his advice and moral support at any moment, and it was only after a bit that I realized that the telephone was ringing.

It was, as I had rather expected it would be, my late father's sister Dahlia, and it was made clear immediately that she had just been hearing from Billy Graham and getting the bad news. In a moving passage in which she referred to him as a double-crossing rat she said that he had formally refused to fulfil his sacred obligations.

'He had some extraordinary story about finding Cook in your cottage with a picture round his neck and a tablecloth over him and of being scared of going near him. Sounded like raving to me.'

'No, it was quite true.'

'You mean he really did have the picture round his neck and the tablecloth over him?'

'Yes.'

'How did he get that way?'

'We had a little argument, and that was how it worked out.'

She snorted in a rather febrile manner.

'Are you telling me that *you* are responsible for the man Graham's cold feet?'

'In a measure, yes. Let me give you a brief account of the episode,' I said, and did so. When I had finished, she spoke again, and her manner was almost calm.

'I might have known that if there was a chance of mucking up these very delicate negotiations, you would spring to the task. Well, as you are the cause of Graham walking out on us, you'll have to take his place.'

I was expecting this. Graham himself, it will be remembered, had made the same suggestion. I was resolved to discourage it from the outset.

'No!' I cried.

'Did you say No?'

'Yes, a thousand times no.'

'Scared, eh?'

'I am not ashamed to admit it.'

'You wouldn't be ashamed to admit practically anything. Where's your pride? Have you forgotten your illustrious ancestors? There was a Wooster at the time of the Crusades who would have won the Battle of Joppa singlehanded, if he hadn't fallen off his horse.'

'I daresay, but –'

'And the one in the Peninsular War. Wellington always used to say he was the best spy he ever had.'

'Quite possible. Nevertheless –'

'You don't want to show yourself worthy of those splendid fellows?'

'Not if it involves crossing Cook's path again.'

'Well, if you won't, you won't. Poor old Tom, how he will have to suffer. And talking of Tom, I had a letter from him this morning. It was all about the superb dinner Anatole had dished up on the previous night. He was absolutely lyrical. I must give it you to read. Apparently Anatole has struck one of these veins of perfection which French chefs do occasionally strike. Tom says in a postscript "How dear Bertie would have enjoyed this".'

I'm pretty shrewd, and I didn't miss the hideous unspoken threat behind her words. She was switching from the iron hand to the hand in the velvet glove, or rather the other way round, and letting me know without being crude about it that if I didn't allow myself to be bent to her will she would put sanctions on me and bar me from Anatole's cooking.

I made the great decision.

'Say no more, old flesh-and-blood,' I said. 'I will return the cat to store. And if while I am doing so Cook jumps out from behind a bush and tears me into a hundred fragments, what of it? It will be merely one more grave among the hills. What did you say?'

'Just "My Hero",' said the aged relative.

CHAPTER SEVENTEEN

I was more to be pitied than censured, mind you, for quailing a bit in the circs. A touch of the wee sleekit cowering beastie is unavoidable when you're up against it as I was. I remember once when I was faced with the task of defying my Aunt Agatha and stoutly refusing to put up her son Thos at my flat for his mid-term holiday from his school and take him (a) to the British Museum (b) to the National Gallery and (c) to a play at the Old Vic by a bloke of the name of Chekhov, Jeeves, in whom I had confided the uneasiness I felt when contemplating the shape of things to come, told me my agitation was quite normal.

'Between the acting of a dreadful thing and the first motion,' he said, 'all the interim is like a phantasma or a hideous dream. The genius and the mortal instruments are then in council and the state of man, like to a little kingdom, suffers the nature of an insurrection.'

I could have put it better myself, but I saw what he meant. At these times your feet are bound to get chilly, and there's nothing you can do about it.

I hid my tremors. A lifetime of getting socks on the jaw from the fist of Fate has made Bertram Wooster's face an inscrutable mask, and no one would have suspected that I was not as calm as an oyster on the half-shell as I started out for Eggesford Court with the cat. But actually, behind those granite features I was far from being tranquil. Indeed, you wouldn't have been wrong in saying that I was as jumpy as the above cat would have been if on hot bricks.

I never know when I'm telling a tale of peril and suspense whether to charge straight ahead or whether to pause from time to time and bung in what is called atmosphere. Some prefer the first way, others the second. For the benefit of the latter I will state that it was a nice evening with gentle breezes blowing and stars peeping out and the scent of growing things and all that, and then I can get down to the *res*.

It was dark when I reached the Cook premises, which suited me, for I had dark work to do. I halted the car about half-way up the drive and took the short cut across country. My best friends would have warned me that I was asking for trouble, and they would have been right. The visibility being poor, the terrain lumpy and the cat wriggling, it was a pretty safe bet that sooner or later I would come a purler. This I did as I approached the stables. I struck a wet patch, my feet slid from under me, the cat shot from my arms, falling to earth I know not where, and I found myself face down in what was unquestionably mud which had been there some time and had had a number of unpleasant substances thrown into it. I remember thinking as I extracted myself that it was lucky I wasn't on my way to mix in company, as that mud must have taken at least eighty per cent off my glamour. It was not Bertram Wooster, the natty boulevardier, who started to return to the car but one of the dregs of society who had got his clothes off a handy scarecrow and had slept in them.

I say 'started to return', for I had not gone more than a yard or two when something solid bumped against my leg and I became aware that I had been joined by a dog of formidable physique, none other than the one I had exchanged civilities with at Wee Nooke. I recognized him by his ears.

At our former meeting, overcome by having found what he instantly recognized as one of the right sort, he had made the welkin ring in his enthusiasm. I urged him in an undertone to preserve a tactful silence now, for you never knew what minions of Pop Cook might be abroad in the night, and my presence would be difficult to explain, but there was no reasoning with him. At Wee Nooke he had found the Wooster aroma roughly equivalent to Chanel Number Five, and it was as if he were trying now to assure me that he was not the dog to be put off a pal just because the pal's scent had deteriorated somewhat. It's the soul that counts, you could hear him saying to himself between barks.

Well, I appreciated the compliment, of course, but I was not my usual debonair self, for I feared the worst. Barking like this, I felt, could not go unheard unless Cook's outdoor staff had been recruited entirely from deaf adders. And I was right. Somewhere off-stage a voice shouted 'Hey', making it clear that Bertram, as so often before, was about to cop it amidships.

I gave the dog a reproachful look. Not much good in that light, of course. I was recalling the story they used to read to me in my childhood, the one about the fellow who had written a book and his dog Diamond chewed up the manuscript; the point being what a decent chap the fellow was, because all he said was 'Ah, Diamond, Diamond, you little know what you have done'. It ought to be 'thou little knowest' and 'what thou hast done', but I can't do the dialect.

I feature the story because I was equally restrained. 'I *told* you not to bark, you silly ass,' was my only comment, and as I spoke the shouter who had shouted 'Hey' came up.

He had not made a good impression on me from the start because his voice had reminded me of the Sergeant-Major who used to come twice a week to drill us at the private school where I won the Scripture Knowledge prize which I may have mentioned once or twice. The Sergeant-Major's voice had been like a vehicle full of tin cans going over gravel, and so was the Hey chap's. Some relation, perhaps.

It was pretty dark, of course, by now, but the visibility was good enough to enable me to see that there was something else I didn't like about this creature of the night – viz. that he was shoving a whacking great shotgun against my midriff. Taken all in all, a bloke to be conciliated with soft speech rather than struck in the mazzard. I tried speech, keeping it as soft as I could manage with my teeth chattering.

'Nice evening,' I said. 'I wonder if you could direct me to the village of Maiden Eggesford,' and would have gone on to explain that I had been for a country ramble and had lost my way, but I don't think he was listening, because all he did was bellow ''Enry', presumably addressing a colleague called Henry something, and a voice that might have been that of the Sergeant-Major's son replied 'Yus?'

'Cummere.'

'Where?'

'Here. Wanteher.'

'I'm having me supper.'

'Well, stop having it and cummere. I've cotched a chap after the horses.'

He had found the right talking-point. Henry was plainly a

man who let nothing stand between him and his duty. When d. called he abandoned his eggs and bacon or whatever it was and hastened to answer the summons. In next to no time he was with us. The dog had disappeared. It was a dog, no doubt, with all sorts of interests and could give only a certain amount of its attention to each. Having sniffed my trouser legs and put his front paws on my chest, he felt that the time had come to seek other fields of endeavour.

Henry had a torch with him. He let it play on me.

'Coo,' he said. 'Is this him?'

'R.'

'Nasty slinking-looking bleeder.'

'R.'

'He don't half niff.'

'R.'

'Brings to mind that old song "It ain't all violets".'

'Lavender.'

'Violets, I always thought.'

'No, lavender.'

'Well, have it your own way. What are you going to do with him?'

'Take him to Mr Cook.'

The prospect of another meeting with Pop Cook under such conditions and after what had occurred between us was naturally distasteful to me, but there seemed little I could do about it, for at this moment Henry attached himself to my collar and we moved off, his associate prodding me in the back with his gun.

They took me to the house, where we were ill received by a butler annoyed at being interrupted while smoking an off-duty pipe. He further resented being confronted with what he called tramps who smelled like something gone wrong with the drains. I didn't know what I had fallen into, but it was becoming abundantly evident that it had been something rather special. The whole tone of the public's reaction to my society emphasized this.

The butler was very definite about everything. No, he said, they couldn't see Mr Cook. Were they under the impression, he asked, that Mr Cook was wearing a gas mask? In any case, he added, even if I had been smelling like new-mown hay, Mr Cook could not be disturbed, because he had a gentleman with him. Shut the fellow up in one of the stables why don't you, the butler said, and this was what my proposer and seconder decided to do.

I cannot too strongly recommend those of my readers who are thinking of getting shut up in stables to abandon the idea, for there is no percentage in it. It's stuffy, it's dark and there's nowhere to sit except the floor. Odd squeaking noises and sinister scratching noises making themselves heard from time to time, suggesting that rats are getting up an appetite before starting to chew you to the bone. After my escort had left me I shuffled about a good deal, with a view to finding some way of removing myself from as morale-testing a position as I had been in since I was so high, but the only method which occurred to me was to catch a rat and train it to gnaw through the door, but that would take time and I was anxious to get home and go to bed.

I had groped my way to the door as I was weighing the pros and cons of this rat sequence, and automatically, my mind on other things, I gave the handle a twiddle, more by way of something to do than because I expected anything to come of it, and shiver my timbers if the door didn't come open.

I thought at first that my guardian angel, who had been noticeably lethargic up to this point, had taken a stiff shot of vitamin something and had become the ball of fire he ought to have been right along, but reflection told me what must have happened. There had been confusion between the two principals, arising from inadequate planning. Each had thought the other had turned the key, with the result that it had remained unturned. It just showed how foolish it is to embark on any enterprise without first having a frank round-table conference conducted in an atmosphere of the utmost cordiality. It was difficult to think which of the two would kick himself harder when it was drawn to their attention that they had lost their Bertram.

But though I was now as free as the air, as you might say, I could see that it behooved me, if behooved is the word I want, to watch my step with the utmost vigilance. It would be too silly to run into Henry and the other bloke again and get bunged into durance-whatever-it's-called once more. I wanted complete freedom from both of them. Probably quite decent chaps when you got to know them, but definitely not for me.

Their sphere of influence was no doubt confined to the stable yard and neighbourhood, so it would be safe to leave by the route I had come by, but I shrank from doing that because I might meet that mud again. The thing to do was to roam about till I found the drive and go down it to where I had left the car. This I proceeded to do, and I had rounded the house and was crossing a lawn of sorts, when something gleamed in front of me and before I could stop myself I was stepping into a swimming-pool.

It was with mixed emotions that I rose to the surface. Surprise was one of them, for I hadn't thought that Cook was the sort of fellow to have a swimming-pool. Another was annoyance. I am not accustomed to bathing with all my clothes on, though there was that occasion at the Drones when Tuppy Glossop betted me I couldn't swing across the pool by the rings and I was reaching the last one when I found he had roped it back, causing me to fall into the fluid in correct evening costume.

But oddly enough, the emotion which stood out from the mixture was one of pleasure. Left to myself, I wouldn't have indulged in these aquatic sports, but now that I was in I was quite enjoying my dip. And there was the agreeable thought that this would do much to reduce the bouquet I had been giving out. What I had needed to enable me to rejoin the human herd without exciting adverse comment had been a good rinsing.

So I did not hurry to leave the pool, but floated there like a water-lily, or perhaps it would be better to say like a dead fish. And I had been doing so for some minutes, when there was that old familiar sound of barking in the night, and I gathered that my friend the dog had found another soul-mate.

I paused in my floating. I didn't like this. It suggested that Henry and his pal the man behind the gun were on the prowl again. What more likely than that they had got together and compared notes about locking the door and rushed to the stable and found me conspic. by my absence? I stiffened till my resemblance to a dead fish was even more striking than it had been, and I was still rigid when I heard the sound of galloping feet, as if somebody in a hurry were coming my way, and a human form splashed into the pool beside me.

That this had not been an intentional move on the human form's part was made clear by his opening remark on rising to the surface. It was the word 'Help!', and I had no difficulty in recognizing the voice of Orlo Porter.

'Help!' he repeated.

'Oh, hullo, Porter,' I said. 'Did you say "Help!"?'

'Yes.'

'Can't you swim?'

'No.'

'Then . . .' I was about to say 'Then surely it was rash to come bathing!', but I refrained, feeling that it would not be tactful. 'Then you could probably do with a helping hand,' I said.

He said he could, and I gave him one. We were at the deep end, and I hauled him into the shallow end, where he immediately became more at his ease. Spitting out perhaps a couple of pints of water, he thanked me – brokenly, as you might say – and I begged him not to mention it.

'Quite a surprise, meeting you like this,' I said. 'What are you doing in these parts, Porter?'

'Call me Orlo.'

'What are you doing in these parts, Orlo? Watching owls?'

'I came to see that blasted Cook, Wooster.'

'Call me Bertie.'

'I came to see that blasted Cook, Bertie. You remember your advice. Approach the old child of unmarried parents after he has had dinner, you said, and the more I thought about it, the sounder the idea seemed. You really have an extraordinary flair, Bertie. You read your fellow man like a book.'

'Oh, thanks. Just a matter of studying the psychology of the individual.'

'Unfortunately you can't judge someone like Cook by ordinary standards. Do you know why this is, Bertie?'

'No, Orlo. Why?'

'Because he's a hellhound, and there's no telling what a hellhound will do. Planning strategy is hopeless when you're dealing with hellhounds.'

'I gather that things did not go altogether as planned.'

'And how right you are, Bertie. The thing was a flop. It couldn't have been a worse flop if I had been trying to get money out of a combination of Scrooge and Gaspard the Miser.'

'Tell me, Orlo.'

'If you have a moment, Bertie.'

'All the time in the world, Orlo.'

'You don't want to hurry away anywhere?'

'No, I like it here.'

'So do I. Pleasantly cool, is it not. Well, then, I arrived and told the butler I wanted to see Mr Cook on a matter of importance, and the butler took me to the library, where I found Cook smoking a fat cigar. I was confident when I saw it that I had chosen my time right. The cigar was plainly an after-dinner cigar, and he was drinking brandy. There could be no doubt that the man was full to the back teeth. You are following me, Bertie?'

'I get the picture, Orlo.'

'There was another man there. Some sort of African explorer, I gathered.'

'Major Plank.'

'His presence was an embarrassment because he would insist on telling us all about the fertility rites of the natives of Bongo on the Congo, which, take it from me, are too improper for words, but he left us after a while and I was able to get down to business. And a lot of good it did me. Cook refused to part with a penny.'

I put a question which had been in my mind for some time. I don't say I had actually been worrying about Orlo's financial position, but it had seemed to me to need explaining.

'What exactly is the arrangement about your money? Surely Cook can't just hang on to it?'

'He can till I'm thirty.'

'How old are you?'

'Twenty-seven.'

'Then in another three years –'

For the first time he showed a flash of the old Orlo Porter who had been so anxious to tear out my insides with his bare hands. He didn't actually foam at the mouth, but I could see that he missed it by the closest of margins.

'But I don't want to wait another three years, dammit. Do you know what my insurance company pays me? A pittance. Barely enough to keep body and soul together on. And I am a man who likes nice things. I want to branch out.'

'A Mayfair flat?'

'Yes.'

'Champagne with every meal?'

'Exactly.'

'Rolls-Royces?'

'Those, too.'

'Leaving something over, of course, to slip to the hard-up proletariat? You'd like them to have what you don't need.'

'There won't be anything I don't need.'

It was a little difficult to know what to say. I had never talked things over with a Communist before, and it came as something of a shock to find that he wasn't so fond of the hard-up proletariat as I had supposed. I thought of advising him not to let the boys at the Kremlin hear him expressing such views, but decided that it was none of my business. I changed the subject.

'By the way, Orlo,' I said, 'what brought you here?'

'Haven't you been listening? I came to see Cook.'

'I mean how did you come to fall into the pool?'

'I didn't know it was there.'

'You seemed to be running very fast. What was your hurry?'

'I was escaping from a dog which was attacking me.'

'A large dog with stand-up ears?'

'Yes. You know it?'

'We've met. But it wasn't attacking you.'

'It sprang on me.'

'In a purely friendly spirit. It springs on everyone. It's its way of being matey.'

He drew a long breath of relief. It would have been longer, had he not lost his footing and disappeared into the depths. I reached about for him and hauled him up, and he thanked me.

'A pleasure,' I said.

'You have taken a weight off my mind, Bertie. I was wondering how I could get back in safety to the inn.'

'I'll give you a lift in my car.'

'No, thanks. Now that you have explained the purity of that dog's motives I'd rather walk. I don't want to catch cold. By the way, Bertie, there's just one point I'd like you to clarify for me. What are *you* doing here?'

'Just strolling around.'

'It struck me as odd that you should have been in the pool.'

'Oh, no. Just cooling off, Orlo, just cooling off.'

'I see. Well, good night, Bertie.'

'Good night, Orlo.'

'I can rely on the accuracy of your information about the dog?'

'Completely, Orlo. His life is gentle, and the elements mixed in him just right,' I said, remembering a gag of Jeeves's.

It was with water dripping from my person in all directions but with a song in my heart, as the expression is, that some minutes later I climbed from the pool and started to where I had left the car. In addition to having a song in it my heart ought of course to have been bleeding for Orlo, for I realized how long it was going to take him to get all those nice things we had been talking about, but the ecstasy of having parted from the cat left little room for sympathy for other people's troubles. My concern for Orlo was, I regret to say, about equal to his for the hard-up proletariat.

All was quiet on the Cook front. No sign of Henry and his pal. The dog after fraternizing with Orlo had apparently curled up somewhere and was getting his eight hours.

I drove on. The song in my heart rose to fortissimo as I got out of the car at the door of Wee Nooke, only to die away in a gurgle as something soft and furry brushed against my leg and looking down I saw the familiar form of the cat.

CHAPTER EIGHTEEN

I should have to check with Jeeves, but I think the word to describe the way I slept that night is 'fitfully'. I turned and twisted like an adagio dancer, and no wonder, for what I have heard Jeeves call 'the fell clutch of circumstance' which was clutching me was not the ordinary fell clutch which can be wriggled out of by some simple ruse such as going on a voyage round the world and not showing up again till things have blown over.

I had the option, of course, of disassociating myself entirely from the cat sequence and refusing to have anything more to do with the ruddy animal, but this would mean Colonel Briscoe scratching Simla's nomination, which would mean that a loved aunt would lose a packet and have to touch Uncle Tom to make up the deficit, which would mean upsetting the latter's gastric juices for one didn't know how long, which would mean him pushing his plate away untasted night after night, which would mean Anatole, temperamental like all geniuses, getting deeply offended and handing in his resignation. Ruin, desolation and despair all round, in short.

Manifestly, I think it's manifestly, the chivalry of the Woosters could not permit all that to happen. Somehow, whatever the perils involved, the cat had to be decanted somewhere where it could find its way back to its GHQ. But who was to do the decanting? Billy Graham had made it plain that no purse of gold, however substantial, could persuade him to brave the horrors of Eggesford Court, that sinister house. Jeeves had formally declared himself a non-starter. And Aunt Dahlia was disqualified by her unfortunate inability to move from spot to spot without having twigs snap beneath her feet.

This put the issue squarely up to Bertram. And no chance for him to do a *nolle prosequi*, because if he did bang went his hopes, for quite a time at least, of enjoying Anatole's cooking.

It was consequently in sombre mood that I went across to the Goose and Grasshopper for breakfast. I do not as a rule take the morning meal at six-thirty, but I had been awake since four, and the pangs of hunger could be resisted no longer.

If there was one thing I had taken for granted, it was that I would be breakfasting alone. My surprise, therefore, at finding Orlo in the dining-room, tucking into eggs and bacon, was considerable. I couldn't imagine how he came to be in circulation at such an hour. Bird-watchers, of course, are irregular in their habits, but even if he had an appointment with a Clarkson's warbler you would have expected him to have made it for much nearer lunch.

'Oh, hullo, Bertie,' he said. 'Glad to see you.'

'You're up early, Orlo.'

'A little before my usual time. I don't want to keep Vanessa waiting.'

'You've asked her to breakfast?'

'No, she will have had breakfast. Our date was for half-past seven. She may, of course, be late. It depends on how soon she can find the key of the garage.'

'Why does she want the key of the garage?'

'To get the Bentley.'

'Why does she want the Bentley?'

'My dear Bertie, we've got to elope in *something*.'

'Elope?'

'I ought to have explained that earlier. Yes, we're eloping, and thank goodness we've got a fine day for it. Ah, here are your eggs. You'll enjoy them. They're very good at the Goose and Grasshopper. Come, no doubt, from contented hens.'

On seating myself at the table I had ordered eggs, and, as he justly observed, they were excellent. But I dug into them listlessly. I was too bewildered to give them the detached thought they deserved.

'Do you mean to say,' I said, 'that you and Vanessa are e-*lop*-ing?'

'The only sober sensible course to pursue. This comes as a surprise?'

'You could knock me down with a ham sandwich.'

'What seems to be puzzling you?'

'I thought you weren't on speaking terms.'

His response was a hyenaesque guffaw. It was plain that he was feeling his oats to no little extent – quite naturally, of course, Vanessa being the tree on which the fruit of his life hung, as I have heard it described. It made me reflect on the extraordinary extent to which tastes can differ. I, as I have shown, though momentarily attracted by her radiant beauty, had frozen in every limb at the prospect of linking my lot with hers, whereas he was obviously all for it. In just the same way my Uncle Tom dances round in circles if he can get hold at enormous expense of a silver oviform chocolate pot of the

Queen Anne period which I wouldn't be seen in public with. Curious.'

He continued to guffaw.

'You aren't up to the minute with your society gossip, Bertie. That's all a thing of the past. Admittedly relations were at one time strained and harsh words spoken about the colour of my liver, but we had a complete reconciliation last night.'

'Oh, you met her last night?'

'Shortly after I left you. She was taking a stroll preparatory to going to bed and bedewing her pillow with salt tears.'

'Why should she do that?'

'Because she thought she was going to marry you.'

'I see. The fate that is worse than death, you might say.'

'Exactly.'

'Sorry she was troubled.'

'Quite all right. She soon got over it when I told her I had been seeing Cook and demanding my money. When she heard that I had several times thumped the table, her remorse for having called me a sleekit cowering beastie was pitiful. She compared me with heroes of old Greek legend, to their disadvantage, and, to cut a long story short, flung herself into my arms.'

'She must have got wet.'

'Very wet. But she didn't mind that. An emotional girl wouldn't.'

'I suppose not.'

'We then decided to elope. You may be wondering what we're going to live on, but with my salary and a bit of money she has from the will of an aunt we shall be all right. So it was arranged that she should have an early breakfast, go to the garage, pinch the Bentley and put the other cars out of action, leaving Cook for pursuing purposes only the gardener's Ford.'

'That ought to fix him.'

'I think so. It is an excellent car for its purpose, but scarcely adapted to chasing daughters across country. Cook will never catch up with us.'

'Though I don't see what he could do, even if he did catch up with you.'

'You don't? What about that hunting crop of his?'

'Ah, yes, I see what you mean.'

I don't know if he would have developed this theme, but before he could speak there came from the street a musical tooting.

'There she is,' he said, and went out.

So did I. I had no wish to meet Vanessa. I slid out of the back door and returned to Wee Nooke. And I had picked up *By Order Of The Czar* and was hoping to discover what it was that he had ordered, my bet being that a lot of characters with names ending in 'sky' would be off to Siberia before they knew what had hit them, when who should enter hurriedly but Orlo.

He had an envelope in his hand.

'Oh, there you are, Bertie,' he said. 'I can only stop a minute. Vanessa's out there in the car.'

'Ask her to come in.'

'She won't come in. She says it would be too painful for you.'

'What would?'

'Meeting her, you ass. Gazing on her when you knew she is another's.'

'Oh, I see.'

'No sense in giving yourself a lot of agony if you don't have to.'

'Quite.'

'I wouldn't have disturbed you, only I wanted to give you this letter. It's a note I've written to Cook in place of the one Vanessa wrote last night.'

'Oh, she wrote him a note?'

'Yes.'

'To be pinned to her pincushion?'

'That was the idea. But she dropped it somewhere and couldn't be bothered to hunt around for it. So I thought I had better send him a line. If you're running away with a man's daughter, it's only civil to let him know. And I would put the facts before him much better than she would. Girls are apt not to stick to the point when writing letters. With the best intentions in the world they ramble and embroider. A University-trained man like myself who contributes to the *New Statesman* does not fall into this blunder. He is concise. He is lucid.'

'I didn't know you wrote for the *New Statesman*.'

'Occasional letters to the editor. And I rarely fail to enter for the weekly competitions.'

'Absorbing work.'

'Very.'

'I'm a writer of sorts myself. When my Aunt Dahlia was running that paper of hers, *Milady's Boudoir*, I did a piece for it on What The Well-Dressed Man Is Wearing.'

'Did you indeed? Next time we meet you must tell me all about it. Can't stop now. Vanessa's waiting and,' he added as the tooting of a horn broke the morning stillness, 'getting impatient. Here's the letter.'

'You want me to take it to Cook?'

'What do you think I want you to do with it? Get it framed?'

And so saying he legged it like a nymph surprised while bathing, and I picked up my *By Order Of The Czar*.

As I did so I was thinking bitterly that I wished the general public would stop regarding me as an uncomplaining Hey-You on whom all the unpleasant jobs could be shovelled off. Whenever something sticky was afoot and action had to be taken the cry was sure to go up, 'Let Wooster do it'. I have already touched on my Aunt Agatha's tendency to unload her foul son Thos on me at all seasons. My Aunt Dahlia had blotted the sunshine from my life in the matter of the cat. And here was Orlo Porter coolly telling me to take the letter to Cook, as if entering Cook's presence in his present difficult mood wasn't much the same as joining Shadrach, Meshach and Abednego, of whom I had read when I won that Scripture Knowledge prize at my private school, on their way to the burning fiery furnace. What, I asked myself, was to be done?

It was a dilemma which might well have baffled a lesser man, but the whole point about the Woosters is that they are not lesser men. I don't suppose it was more than three-quarters of an hour before the solution flashed on me – viz. to write Cook's name and address on the envelope, stick a stamp on it and post it. Having decided to do this, I returned to my reading.

But everything seemed to conspire today to prevent me making any real progress with *By Order Of The Czar*. Scarcely had I perused a paragraph when the door burst open and I found that I was seeing Cook after all. He was standing on the threshold looking like the Demon King in a pantomime.

With him was Major Plank.

CHAPTER NINETEEN

I have always rather prided myself on being a good host, putting visitors at their ease with debonair smiles and courteous wisecracks, but I am compelled to admit that at the sight of these two I didn't come within a mile of doing so, and the best I could do in the way of wisecracks was a hoarse cry like that of a Pekingese with laryngitis. It was left to Plank to get the conversation going.

'We're in luck, Cook,' he said. 'They haven't started yet. Because if they had,' he added, reasoning closely, 'the bounder wouldn't be here, would he?'

'You're right,' said Cook. Then, addressing me, 'Where is my daughter, you scoundrel?'

'Yes, where is she, rat?' said Plank, and I suddenly came over all calm. From being a Pekingese with throat trouble I turned in a flash into one of those fellows in historical novels who flick a speck of dust from the irreproachable mechlin lace at their wrists preparatory to making the bad guys feel like pieces of cheese. Because with my quick intelligence I had spotted that the parties of the second part had got all muddled up and that I was in a position to score off them as few parties of the second part had ever been scored off.

'Fill me in on two points, Messrs Plank and Cook, if you will be so good,' I said, '(a) Why are you taking up space in my cottage which I require for other purposes, and (b) What the hell are you talking about? What is all this song and dance about daughters?'

'Trying to brazen it out,' said Plank. 'I told you he would. He reminds me of a man I knew in East Africa, who always tried to brazen things out. If you caught him with his fingers in your cigar box, he would say he was just tidying the cigars. Fellow named Abercrombie-Smith, eventually eaten by a crocodile on the Lower Zambezi. But even he had to give up when confronted with overwhelming evidence. Confront this blighter with the overwhelming evidence, Cook.'

'I will,' said Cook, producing an envelope from his pocket. 'I have here a letter from my daughter. Signed "Vanessa".'

'A very important point,' said Plank.

'I will read it to you. "Dear Father. I am going away with the man I love."'

'Let's see him wriggle out of that,' said Plank.

'Yes,' said Cook. 'What have you to say?'

'Merely this,' I riposted. I was thinking how mistaken Orlo had been in asserting that girls rambled when writing letters. Anything more lucid and concise than this one I had never come across. Possibly, I felt, Vanessa, too, was a contributor to the *New Statesman*. 'Cook,' I said, 'you are labouring under a what-d'you-call-it.'

'See!' said Plank. 'Didn't I say he would try to brazen it out?'

'That letter does not refer to me.'

'Are you denying that you are the man my daughter loves?'

'That's just what I am denying.'

'In spite of the fact that she is always in and out of this

beastly cottage and is probably at this moment hiding under the bed in the spare room,' said Plank, continuing to shove his oar in in the most unnecessary manner. These African explorers have no tact, no reticence.

'May I explain,' I said. 'The chap you're looking for is Orlo Porter. They fell for each other when she was in London and love has been burgeoning ever since, if burgeoning means what I think it means, until they felt they could bear being separated no longer. So she pinched your car and they've driven off together to the registrar's.'

It didn't go well. Cook said I was lying, and Plank said of course I was, adding that the more he saw of me the more I reminded him of Abercrombie-Smith, who, he said, would undoubtedly have done a long stretch in chokey if the crocodile hadn't taken things into its own hands.

I should have mentioned that in the course of these exchanges Cook's complexion had been steadily deepening. It now looked like a Drone Club tie, which is a rich purple. There was talk at one time of having it crimson with white spots, but the supporters of that view were outvoted.

'How dare you have the insolence to suppose that I am fool enough to believe this story of my daughter being in love with Orlo Porter?' he thundered. 'As if any girl in her senses would love Orlo Porter.'

'Ridiculous,' said Plank.

'Vanessa would turn from him in disgust.'

'On her heel,' said Plank.

'What she can see in *you* I cannot imagine.'

'Nor can I,' said Plank. 'He's got a beard like one of those Victorian novelists. Revolting spectacle.'

It was true that I hadn't shaved this morning, but this was

going too far. I don't mind criticism, but I will not endure vulgar abuse.

'Pfui,' I said. It is an expression I don't often use, but Nero Wolfe is always saying it with excellent results, and it seemed to fit in rather well here. 'Enough of this back-chat. Read this,' I said, handing Cook Orlo's letter.

I must say his reception of what Plank would have called the overwhelming evidence was all that could be desired. His jaw fell. He snorted. His face crumpled up like a sheet of carbon paper.

'Good God!' he gurgled.

'What is it?' asked Plank. 'What's the matter?'

'This is from Porter, saying that he has eloped with Vanessa.'

'Probably a forgery.'

'No. Porter's writing is unmistakable . . .' He choked. 'Mr Wooster –'

'Don't call him Mister Wooster as if he were a respectable member of society,' said Plank. 'He's a desperate criminal who once came within an ace of stinging me for five pounds. He is known to the police as Alpine Joe. Address him as that. Wooster is only a pen name.'

Cook did not seem to have listened – and I didn't blame him.

'Mr Wooster, I owe you an apology.'

I decided to temper justice with m. No sense in grinding the poor old buster beneath the iron heel. True, he had been extremely offensive, but to a man who has lost his daughter and his cat within a day or two of each other much must be excused.

'Don't give it another thought, my dear fellow,' I said. 'We all make mistakes. I forgive you freely. If this little misunder-standing has taught you not to speak till you are sure of your facts, it will have been time well spent.'

I had paused, speculating as to whether I wasn't being a bit too patronizing, when somebody said 'Miaow' in a low voice, and looking down I saw that the cat had strolled in. And if ever a cat chose the wrong moment for getting the party spirit and wanting to mix with the boys, this cat was that cat. I looked at it with a wild surmise, as silent as those bimbos on the peak in Darien. With both hands pressed to the top of my head to prevent it taking to itself the wings of a dove and soaring to the ceiling, I was asking myself what the harvest would be.

I was speedily informed on this point.

'Ha!' said Cook, scooping up the animal and pressing it to his bosom. He seemed to have lost all interest in eloping daughters.

'I told you it must have been Alpine Joe who was the kidnapper,' said Plank. 'That was why he was hanging about the stables that day. He was waiting his chance.'

'Biding his time.'

'And he hasn't a word to say for himself.'

He was right. I was unable to utter. I couldn't clear myself by exposing the aged relative at the bar of world opinion. I couldn't make them believe that I was going to return the cat. You might have described me as being trapped in the net of fate if you had happened to think of the expression, and when that happens to you, it is no use saying anything. Ask the boys in Dartmoor or Pentonville. I could only trust that joy at recovering his lost one might soften Cook's heart and make him let me off lightly.

Not a hope.

'I shall insist on an exemplary sentence,' he said.

'And meanwhile,' said Plank in that offensively officious way of his, 'shall I be hitting him on the head with my stick? The Zulu knob-kerrie would be better, but I left it up at the house.'

'I was going to ask you to go for a policeman.'

'While you do what?'

'While I take the cat back to Potato Chip.'

'Suppose while we're both gone he does a bunk?'

'You have a point there.'

'When anyone is caught stealing in Bongo on the Congo, they tie him down on an ant-hill until they can get hold of the walla-walla, as judges are called in the native dialect. Makes it awkward for the accused if he isn't fond of ants and the walla-walla is away for the week-end, but into each life some rain must fall and he ought to have thought of that before he started pinching things. We're short of ants, of course, but we can tie him to the sofa. It only means pulling down a couple of curtain cords.'

'Then by all means let us do as you suggest.'

'Better gag him. We don't want him yelling for help.'

'My dear Plank, you think of everything.'

I am a great reader of novels of suspense, and I had often wondered how the heroes of them felt when the heavy tied them up, as he generally did about half-way through. I was now in a position to get a rough idea, but of course only a rough one, for they were pretty nearly always attached to a barrel of gunpowder with a lighted candle on top of it, which must have made the whole thing considerably more poignant.

I had been spared this what you might call added attraction, but even so I was far from being in sunny mood. I think it was the gag which contributed most to the lowering of my spirits. Plank had inserted his tobacco pouch between my upper and lower teeth, and it tasted far too strongly of African explorer to be agreeable. It was a great relief when I heard a footstep and realized that Jeeves had returned from revelling with Mrs P. B. Pigott of Balmoral, Mafeking Road.

'Good morning, sir,' he said.

He expressed no surprise at seeing me tied to a sofa with curtain cords, just as he would have e. no s. if he had seen me being eaten by a crocodile like the late Abercrombie-Smith, though in the latter case he might have heaved a regretful sigh.

Assuming that I would prefer to be without them, he removed the gag and unfastened my bonds.

'Have you breakfasted, sir?' he asked. I told him I had.

'Perhaps some coffee, sir?'

'A great idea. And make it strong,' I said, hoping that it would wash the taste of Plank's tobacco pouch away. 'And when you return, I shall a tale unfold which will make you jump as if you'd sat on a fretful porpentine.'

I was quite wrong, of course. I doubt if he would do much more than raise an eyebrow if, when entering his pantry, he found one of those peculiar fauna from the Book of Revelations in the sink. When he returned with the steaming pot and I unfolded my tale, he listened attentively, but gave no indication that he recognized that what he was listening to was front page stuff. Only when I told him of the clicking of Orlo and Vanessa, releasing me from my honourable obligations to the latter, did a flicker of interest disturb his frozen features. I think he might have unbent to the extent of offering me respectful congratulations, had not Plank come bounding in.

He was alone. I could have told him it was hopeless to try to get hold of the Maiden Eggesford Police Force at that time of day. There was only one of it and in the morning he does his rounds on his bicycle.

Seeing Jeeves, he registered astonishment.

'Inspector Witherspoon!' he cried. 'Amazing how you Scotland Yard fellows always get your man. I suppose you've been on Alpine Joe's trail for weeks like a stoat and a rabbit. Little did he know that Inspector Witherspoon, the man who never sleeps, was watching his every move. Well, you couldn't have come up with him at a better moment, for in addition to whatever the police want him for he has stolen a valuable cat belonging to my friend Cook. We caught him redhanded, or as redhanded as it is possible to be when stealing cats. But I'm surprised that you should have untied him from the sofa. I always thought the one thing the police were fussy about was the necessity of leaving everything untouched.'

I must say I was what is called at a loss of words, but luckily Jeeves had plenty.

'I fail to understand you,' he said, his voice and manner so chilly that Plank must have been wishing he was wearing his winter woollies. 'And may I ask why you address me as Inspector Witherspoon? I am not Inspector Witherspoon.'

Plank clicked his tongue impatiently.

'Of course you are,' he said. 'I remember you distinctly. You'll be telling me next that you didn't arrest this man at my place in Gloucestershire for trying to obtain five pounds from me by false pretences.'

Jeeves had no irreproachable mechlin lace at his wrist, or he would unquestionably have flicked a speck of dust off it. He increased the coldness of his manner.

'You are mistaken in every respect,' he said. 'Mr Wooster has ample means. It seems scarcely likely, therefore, that he would have attempted to obtain a mere five pounds from you. I can speak with authority as to Mr Wooster's financial standing, for I am his solicitor and prepare his annual income tax return.'

'So there you are, Plank,' I said. 'It must be obvious to every thinking man that you have been having hallucinations, possibly the result of getting a touch of the sun while making a pest of yourself to the natives of Equatorial Africa. If I were you, I'd pop straight back to E. J. Murgatroyd and have him give you something for it. You don't want that sort of thing to spread. You'll look silly if it goes too far and we have to bury you before sundown.'

Plank was plainly shaken. He could not pale beneath his tan because he had so much tan that it was impossible to pale beneath it. I'm not sure I have put that exactly right. What I mean is that he may have paled, but you couldn't see it because of his sunburn.

But he was looking very thoughtful, and I knew what was passing in his mind. He was wondering how he was going to explain to Cook, whom by tying people to sofas he had rendered liable for heavy damages for assault and battery and all sorts of things.

These African explorers think quick. It took him about five seconds flat to decide not to stay and explain to Cook. Then he was out of the room in a flash, his destination presumably Bongo on the Congo or somewhere similar where the arm of the law couldn't touch him. I don't suppose he had shown a brisker turn of speed since the last time he had thought the natives seemed friendly and had decided to stay the night, only to have them come after him with assegais.

My first move after he had left us was, of course, to pay a marked tribute to Jeeves for his services and co-operation. This done, we struck the more social note.

'Did you have a good time last night, Jeeves?'

'Extremely enjoyable, thank you, sir.'

'How was your aunt?'

'At first somewhat dispirited.'

'Why was that?'

'She had lost her cat, sir. On leaving for her holiday she placed it in the charge of a friend, and it had strayed.'

I gasped. A sudden idea had struck me. We Woosters are like that. We are always getting struck by sudden ideas.

'Jeeves! Could it be . . . Do you think it's possible . . . ?'

'Yes, sir. She described the animal to me in minute detail, and there can be no doubt that it is the one now in residence at Eggesford Court.'

I danced a carefree dance step. I know a happy ending when I see one.

'Then we've got Cook cold!'

'So it would seem, sir.'

'We go to him and tell him he can carry on plus cat till the race is over, paying, of course, a suitable sum to your aunt. Lend-lease, isn't it called?'

'Yes, sir.'

'And in addition we make it a proviso . . . It is proviso?'

'Yes, sir.'

'That he gives Orlo Porter his money. I'd like to see Orlo fixed up. He can't refuse, because he must have the cat, and if he tries any *nolle prosequi* as regards Orlo we slap an assault and battery suit on him. Am I right, Jeeves?'

'Indubitably, sir.'

'And another thing. I have thought for some time that the hectic rush and swirl of life in Maiden Eggesford can scarcely be what E. Jimpson Murgatroyd had in mind when he sent me to the country to get a complete rest. What I need is something quieter, more peaceful, as it might be in New York. And if I am mugged, what of it? It is probably all right getting mugged, when you are used to it. Do you agree, Jeeves?'

'Yes, sir.'

'And you are in favour of bearding Pop Cook?'

'Yes, sir.'

'Then let's go. My car is outside. Next stop, Eggesford Court.'

It was about a week after we had fetched up in New York that coming to the breakfast table one morning, rejoicing in my youth if I remember rightly, I found a letter with an English stamp lying by my plate. Not recognizing the writing, I pushed it aside, intending to get at it later after I had fortified myself with a square meal. I generally do this with the letters I get at breakfast time, because if they're stinkers and you read them on an empty stomach, you start your day all wrong. And in these disturbed times you don't often find people writing anything but stinkers.

Some half-hour later, refreshed and strengthened, I opened the envelope, and no wonder the writing had seemed unfamiliar, for it was from Uncle Tom, and he hadn't written to me since I was at my private school, when, to do him credit, he had always enclosed a postal order for five or ten bob.

He hauled up his slacks thus:

Dear Bertie.

You will doubtless be surprised at hearing from me. I am writing for your aunt, who has met with an unfortunate accident and is compelled to wear her arm in a sling. This occurred during the concluding days of her visit to some friends of hers in Somerset named Briscoe. If I understand her rightly, a party was in progress to celebrate the victory of Colonel Briscoe's horse Simla in an important race, and a cork, extracted from a bottle of champagne, struck her so sharply on the tip of the nose that she lost her balance and fell, injuring her wrist.

Then came three pages about the weather, the income tax (which he dislikes) and the recent purchases he had made for his collection of old silver, and finally a postscript:

PS Your aunt asks me to enclose this newspaper clipping.

I couldn't find any newspaper clipping, and I supposed he must have forgotten to enclose it. Then I saw it lying on the floor.

I picked it up. It was from the *Bridmouth Argus*, with which is incorporated the *Somerset Farmer* and the *South Country Intelligencer*, the organ, if you remember, whose dramatic critic gave the old ancestor such a rave notice when she sang 'Every Nice Girl Loves A Sailor' in her sailor suit at the Maiden Eggesford village concert.

It ran as follows:

JUBILEE STAKES SENSATION
JUDGES' DECISION

Yesterday the Judges, Major Welsh, Admiral Sharpe and Sir Everard Boot, after prolonged consideration, gave their decision in the Jubilee Stakes incident which has led to so much controversy in Bridmouth-on-Sea sporting circles. The race was awarded to Colonel Briscoe's Simla. Bets will accordingly be settled in accordance with this *fiat*. Rumour whispers that large sums will change hands.

Here I paused, for letter and clipping had given me much food for thought.

Naturally it was with the deepest concern that I pictured the tragic scene of Aunt Dahlia and the champagne cork. Something similar happened to me once during some rout or revelry at the Drones, and I can testify that it calls for all that one has of fortitude. But against this must be set the fact that she had won a substantial chunk of money and would not be faced with the awful necessity of getting into Uncle Tom's ribs in order to keep the budget balanced.

But this aspect of the matter ceased to enchain my interest. What I wanted was to probe to the heart of the mystery that had presented itself. Apparently Cook's Potato Chip had finished first but had been disqualified. Why? Bumping?

That's usually what you get disqualified for.

I read on.

The facts will of course be fresh in the minds of our readers. Rounding into the straight, Simla and his rival were neck and neck, far ahead of the field, and it was plain that one of the two must be the ultimate winner. Nearing the finish, Simla took the lead and was a full length ahead, when a cat with black and white markings suddenly ran on to the course, causing him to shy and unseat his jockey.

It was then discovered that the cat was the property of Mr Cook and had actually been brought to the course in his horse's horse box. It was this that decided the judges, who, as we say, yesterday awarded the race to Colonel Briscoe's entrant. Sympathy has been expressed for Mr Cook.

Not by me, I hasten to say. I felt it served the old blighter jolly well right. He ought to have known that you can't go about the place for years making a hellhound of yourself without eventually paying the price. Remember what the fellow said about the mills of the gods.

I was in philosophical mood as I smoked the after-breakfast cigarette. Jeeves came in to clear away the debris, and I told him the news.

'Simla won, Jeeves.'

'Indeed, sir? That is most gratifying.'

'And Aunt Dahlia got hit on the tip of the nose with a champagne cork.'

'Sir?'

'At the subsequent celebrations at the Briscoe home.'

'Ah, yes, sir. A painful experience, but no doubt satisfaction at her financial gains would enable Mrs Travers to bear it with fortitude. Was the tone of her communication cheerful?'

'The letter wasn't from her, it was from Uncle Tom. He enclosed this.'

I handed him the clipping, and I could see how deeply it interested him. One of his eyebrows rose at least a sixteenth of an inch.

'Dramatic, Jeeves.'

'Exceedingly, sir. But I am not sure that I altogether agree with the verdict of the judges.'

'You don't?'

'I should have been inclined to regard the episode as an Act of God.'

'Well, thank goodness the decision wasn't up to you. The imagination boggles at the thought of how Aunt Dahlia would have reacted if it had gone the other way. One pictures her putting hedgehogs in Major Welsh's bed and getting fourteen days without the option for pouring buckets of water out of windows on the heads of Admiral Sharpe and Sir Everard Boot. I should have got nervous prostration in the first couple of days. And it was difficult enough to avoid nervous prostration in Maiden Eggesford as it was, Jeeves,' I said, my philosophical mood now buzzing along on all twelve cylinders. 'Do you ever brood on life?'

'Occasionally, sir, when at leisure.'

'What do you make of it? Pretty odd in spots, don't you think?'

'It might be so described, sir.'

'This business of such-and-such seeming to be so-and-so, when it really isn't so-and-so at all. You follow me?'

'Not entirely, sir.'

'Well, take a simple instance. At first sight Maiden Eggesford had all the indications of being a haven of peace. You agreed with me?'

'Yes, sir.'

'As calm and quiet as you could wish, with honeysuckle-covered cottages and apple-cheeked villagers wherever you looked. Then it tore off its whiskers and revealed itself as an inferno. To obtain calm and quiet we had to come to New York, and there we got it in full measure. Life saunters along on an even keel. Nothing happens. Have we been mugged?'

'No, sir.'

'Or shot by youths?'

'No, sir.'

'No, sir, is right. We are tranquil. And I'll tell you why. There are no aunts here. And in particular we are three thousand miles away from Mrs Dahlia Travers of Brinkley Manor, Market Snodsbury, Worcestershire. Don't get me wrong, Jeeves, I love the old flesh-and-blood. In fact I revere her. Nobody can say she isn't good company. But her moral code is lax. She cannot distinguish between what is according to Hoyle and what is not according to Hoyle. If she wants to do anything, she doesn't ask herself "Would Emily Post approve of this?", she goes ahead and does it, as she did in this matter of the cat. Do you know what is the trouble with aunts as a class?'

'No, sir.'

'They are not gentlemen,' I said gravely.

P. G. Wodehouse

IN ARROW BOOKS

If you have enjoyed Jeeves and Wooster, you'll love Blandings

FROM

Service with a Smile

I

The morning sun shone down on Blandings Castle, and the various inmates of the ancestral home of Clarence, ninth Earl of Emsworth, their breakfasts digested, were occupying themselves in their various ways. One may as well run through the roster just to keep the record straight.

Beach, the butler, was in his pantry reading an Agatha Christie; Voules, the chauffeur, chewing gum in the car outside the front door. The Duke of Dunstable, who had come uninvited for a long visit and showed no signs of ever leaving, sat spelling through *The Times* on the terrace outside the amber drawing-room, while George, Lord Emsworth's grandson, roamed the grounds with the camera which he had been given on his twelfth birthday. He was photographing – not that the fact is of more than mild general interest – a family of rabbits down by the west wood.

Lord Emsworth's sister, Lady Constance, was in her boudoir writing a letter to her American friend James Schoonmaker. Lord Emsworth's secretary, Lavender Briggs, was out looking for Lord Emsworth. And Lord Emsworth himself, accompanied by Mr Schoonmaker's daughter Myra, was on his way to the headquarters of Empress of Blandings, his pre-eminent sow, three times silver medallist in the Fat Pigs class at the Shropshire Agricultural Show. He had taken the girl with him because it seemed to him that she was a trifle on the low-spirited side these days, and he knew from his own experience that there was nothing like an after-breakfast look at the Empress for bracing one up and bringing the roses back to the cheeks.

'There is her sty,' he said, pointing a reverent finger as they crossed the little meadow dappled with buttercups and daisies. 'And that is my pigman Wellbeloved standing by it.'

Myra Schoonmaker, who had been walking with bowed head, as if pacing behind the coffin of a dear and valued friend, glanced listlessly in the direction indicated. She was a pretty girl of the small, slim, slender type, who would have been prettier if she had been more cheerful. Her brow was furrowed, her lips drawn, and the large brown eyes which rested on George Cyril Wellbeloved had in them something of the sadness one sees in those of a dachshund which, coming to the dinner table to get its ten per cent, is refused a cut off the joint.

'Looks kind of a plugugly,' she said, having weighed George Cyril in the balance.

'Eh? What? What?' said Lord Emsworth, for the word was new to him.

'I wouldn't trust a guy like that an inch.'

Enlightenment came to Lord Emsworth.

'Ah, you have heard, then, how he left me some time ago and went to my neighbour, Sir Gregory Parsloe. Outrageous and disloyal, of course, but these fellows will do these things. You don't find the old feudal spirit nowadays. But all that is in the past, and I consider myself very fortunate to have got him back. A most capable man.'

'Well, I still say I wouldn't trust him as far as I can throw an elephant.'

At any other moment it would have interested Lord Emsworth to ascertain how far she could throw an elephant, and he would have been all eager questioning. But with the Empress awaiting him at journey's end he was too preoccupied to go into the matter. As far as he was capable of hastening, he hastened on, his mild eyes gleaming in anticipation of the treat in store.

Propping his back against the rail of the sty, George Cyril Wellbeloved watched him approach, a silent whistle of surprise on his lips.

'Well, strike me pink!' he said to his immortal soul. 'Cor chase my aunt Fanny up a gum tree!'

What had occasioned this astonishment was the fact that his social superior, usually the sloppiest of dressers and generally regarded as one of Shropshire's more prominent eyesores, was now pure Savile Row from head to foot. Not even the *Tailor and Cutter's* most acid critic could have found a thing to cavil at in the quiet splendour of his appearance. Enough to startle any beholder accustomed to seeing him in baggy flannel trousers, an old shooting coat with holes in the elbows, and a hat which would have been rejected disdainfully by the least fastidious of tramps.

It was no sudden outbreak of foppishness that had wrought this change in the ninth earl's outer crust, turning him into a prismatic sight at which pigmen blinked amazed. As he had explained to Myra Schoonmaker on encountering her mooning about in the hall, he was wearing the beastly things because he was going to London on the 10.35 train, because his sister Connie had ordered him to attend the opening of

Parliament. Though why Parliament could not get itself opened without his assistance he was at a loss to understand.

A backwoods peer to end all backwoods peers, Lord Emsworth had a strong dislike for London. He could never see what pleasure his friend Ickenham found in visiting that frightful city. The latter's statement that London brought out all the best in him and was the only place where his soul could expand like a blossoming flower and his generous nature find full expression bewildered him. Himself he wanted nothing but Blandings Castle, even though his sister Constance, his secretary Lavender Briggs and the Duke of Dunstable were there and Connie, overriding his veto, had allowed the Church Lads' Brigade to camp out by the lake. Many people are fond of church lads, but he was not of their number, and he chafed at Connie's highhandedness in letting loose on his grounds and messuages what sometimes seemed to him about five hundred of them, all squealing simultaneously.

But this morning there was no room in his mind for morbid thoughts about these juvenile pluguglies. He strongly suspected that it was one of them who had knocked his top hat off with a crusty roll at the recent school treat, but with a visit to the Empress in view he had no leisure to brood of past wrongs. One did not think of mundane things when about to fraternize with that wonder-pig.

Arriving at her G.H.Q., he beamed on George Cyril Wellbeloved as if on some spectacle in glorious technicolor. And this was odd, for the O.C. Pigs, as Myra Schoonmaker had hinted, was no feast for the eye, having a sinister squint, a broken nose acquired during a political discussion at the Goose and Gander in Market Blandings, and a good deal of mud all over him. He also smelt rather strongly. But what enchanted Lord Emsworth, gazing on this son of the soil, was not his looks or the bouquet he diffused but his mere presence. It thrilled him to feel that this prince of pigmen was back again, tending the Empress once more. George Cyril might rather closely resemble someone for whom the police were spreading a drag-net in the expectation of making an arrest shortly, but nobody could deny his great gifts. He knew his pigs.

So Lord Emsworth beamed, and when he spoke did so with what, when statesmen meet for conferences, is known as the utmost cordiality.

'Morning, Wellbeloved.'

'Morning, m'lord.'

'Empress all right?'

'In the pink, m'lord.'

'Eating well?'

'Like a streak, m'lord.'

'Splendid. It is so important,' Lord Emsworth explained to Myra Schoonmaker, who was regarding the noble animal with a dull eye, 'that her appetite should remain good. You have of course read your Wolff-Lehmann and will remember that, according to the Wolff-Lehmann feeding standards, a pig, to enjoy health, must consume daily nourishment amounting to fifty-seven thousand eight hundred calories, these to consist of proteids four pounds five ounces, carbohydrates twenty-five pounds.'

'Oh?' said Myra.

'Linseed meal is the secret. That and potato peelings.'

'Oh?' said Myra.

'I knew you would be interested,' said Lord Emsworth. 'And of course skimmed milk. I've got to go to London for a couple of nights, Wellbeloved. I leave the Empress in your charge.'

'Her welfare shall be my constant concern, m'lord.'

'Capital, capital, capital,' said Lord Emsworth, and would probably have gone on doing so for some little time, for he was a man who, when he started saying 'Capital', found it hard to stop, but at this moment a new arrival joined their little group, a tall, haughty young woman who gazed on the world through harlequin glasses of a peculiarly intimidating kind. She regarded the ninth earl with the cold eye of a governess of strict views who has found her young charge playing hooky.

'Pahdon me,' she said.

Her voice was as cold as her eye. Lavender Briggs disapproved of Lord Emsworth, as she did of all those who employed her, particularly Lord Tilbury of the Mammoth Publishing Company, who had been Lord Emsworth's predecessor. When holding a secretarial post, she performed her duties faithfully, but it irked her to be a wage slave. What she wanted was to go into business for herself as the proprietress of a typewriting bureau. It was the seeming impossibility of ever obtaining the capital for this venture that interfered with her sleep at night and in the daytime made her manner more than a little forbidding. Like George Cyril Wellbeloved, whose views were strongly communistic, which was how he got that broken nose, she eyed the more wealthy of her circle askance. Idle rich, she sometimes called them.

Lord Emsworth, who had been scratching the Empress's back with the ferrule of his stick, an attention greatly appreciated by the silver medallist, turned with a start, much as the Lady of Shalott must have turned when the curse came upon her. There was always something about his secretary's voice, when it addressed him unexpectedly, that gave him the feeling that he was a small boy again and had been caught by the authorities stealing jam.

'Eh, what? Oh, hullo, Miss Briggs. Lovely morning.'

'Quate. Lady Constance desiah-ed me to tell you that you should be getting ready to start, Lord Emsworth.'

'What? What? I've plenty of time.'

'Lady Constance thinks othahwise.'

'I'm all packed, aren't I?'

'Quate.'

'Well, then.'

'The car is at the door, and Lady Constance desiah-ed me to tell you –'

'Oh, all right, all right,' said Lord Emsworth peevishly, adding a third 'All right' for good measure. 'Always something, always something,' he muttered, and told himself once again that, of all the secretarial assistants he had had, none, not even the Efficient Baxter of evil memory, could compare in the art of taking the joy out of life with this repellent female whom Connie in her arbitrary way had insisted on engaging against his strongly expressed wishes. Always after him, always harrying him, always popping up out of a trap and wanting him to *do* things. What with Lavender Briggs, Connie, the Duke and those beastly boys screaming and yelling beside the lake, life at Blandings Castle was becoming insupportable.

Gloomily he took one last, lingering look at the Empress and pottered off, thinking, as so many others had thought before him, that the ideal way of opening Parliament would be to put a bomb under it and press the button.